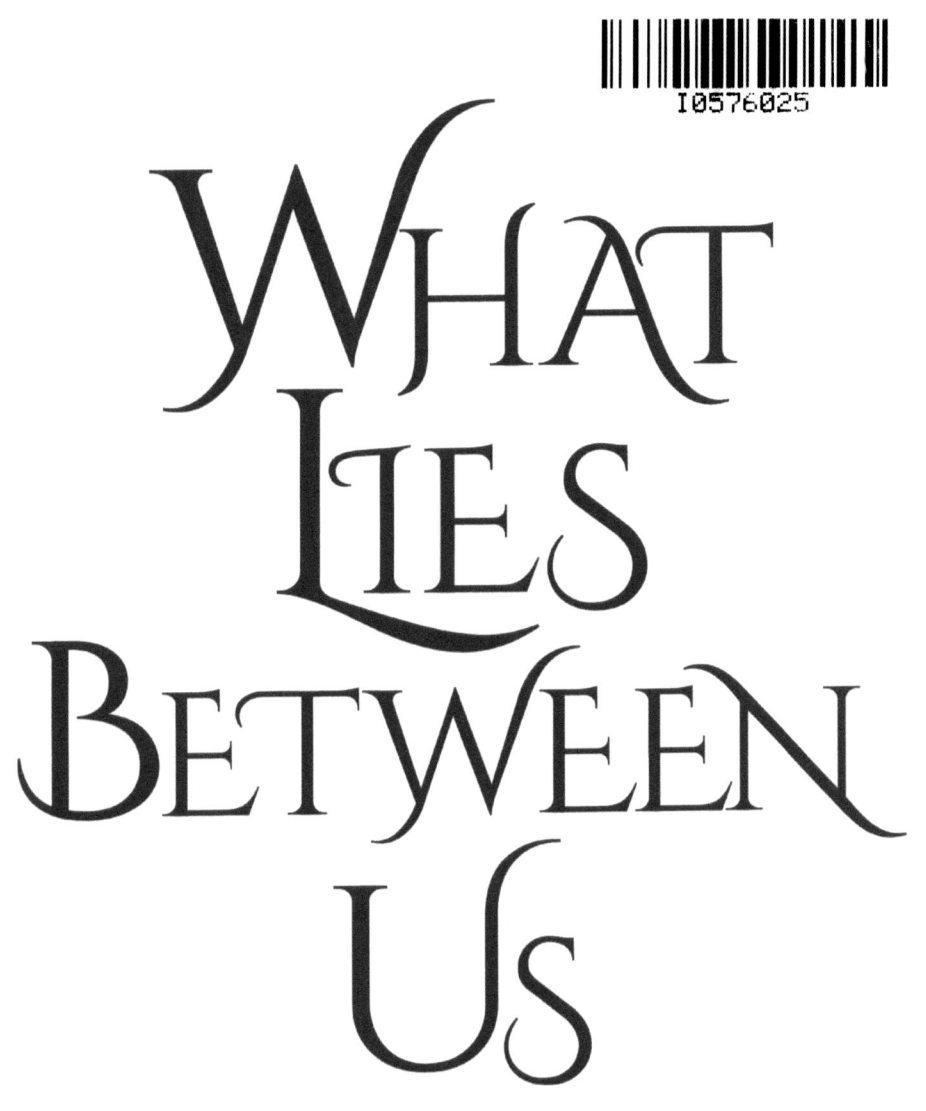

What Lies Between Us

Andi Black

Content warning:
No story is more important than your mental health. Please take a
moment to read over the list of content warnings, and decide if this is
the book for you.
Kidnapping
Torture
Explicit language
Mature content
Parent death
Fighting

Contact: Authorandiblack@gmail.com
Editor: Page Perfectors
Cover Art: Wonky Lines
Blurb: Mckenna Albert

DEDICATION

"Make the most of yourself, for that is all there is of you."
- Ralph Waldo Emerson

PLAYLIST

Coming Down- Dum Dum Girls
Vienna- Billy Joel
Time Of The Season- Roses and Revolutions
In Your head- Cloudyfield
The Prophecy- Taylor Swift
Look After You- The Fray
Crazy in love- The Eden Project
Hear You Me- Jimmy Eat World
Alkaline- Sleep Token
Nothing's Gonna Hurt You Baby- Cigarettes After Sex
As The World Caves In- Matt Maltesse
Heavy Is The Crown- Mike Shinoda and Emily Armstrong
Exit Music For A Film- Radiohead

ACKNOWLEDGEMENTS:

First, to the readers-
Thank you for giving Cairo's story a chance. Writing this book has pushed me out of every comfort zone I have ever had, but it has also shown me the incredible community of readers that exist in the world.

The support and love I've received has been truly amazing, and I am so grateful to my beta readers, the indie author community, and all of the lovely people who found me at the beginning of this journey and have been here ever since. I can't wait to go back to Hadeon and give you all the next story.

Okay, let's get to the sappy stuff-

To my baby sister-
I can't thank you enough for helping me get here. All the hours you spent sitting on the floor plotting ideas with me, the blocks of cheese and whiteboard doodles, the field trips and boiled peanuts, and every brainstorming session we had in my car, all pushed me to get to this point. From day one, you have been my biggest motivator to see this through. I told you I wanted to write a book and you were immediately on board, and you stayed with me the entire time with an unwavering faith that I could and would do it.

There was never a single moment of hesitation from you, only pride and excitement that mirrored my own and soothed my doubts like a salve.

This book would not exist without you.
I love you, swab.
Thank you for believing in me.

To my husband, who endured months of falling asleep to the serene sound of my keyboard clack-clack-clacking in bed next to him, single-handedly bankrolled this entire endeavor, and never once complained, thank you. For the never-ending support in everything I pursue, for the unconditional love and support you've shown me over the last twelve years, and for the safe space you've created that allows me to chase every dream I have. I love you big.

For my boys- I don't know that I could ever let you read this book unless I ripped a few chapters out, but regardless I hope you see this and know that it is never too late, too hard, or too far out of reach for you to chase any dream you have.

You can do or be anything in this world.

I love you all to the moon and back.

A huge thank you to my editor, cover designer, formatter and blurb writer. Each of you had a hand in bringing Cairo's story to life and I am forever grateful for your contributions to this story, and the opportunity to know each of you.

CHAPTER 1:
CAIRO

O rphaned.
Is it still called that if your parents die when you're an adult? The word had been echoing through my mind since I got the phone call, each syllable like a paper cut against my skin. An incessant reminder that I was now completely alone in this world. No siblings, no grandparents. Just me and the only two things I could be certain of right now: one, both of my parents were dead, and now so was my stepfather, and two, there was no one else to deal with the paperwork that comes from someone passing. So there I was, sitting in a tiny lawyer's office in my hometown and waiting for the details of his will.

Heavy sheets of rain fell outside, peppering the window and filling the silence in the room as Mr. Pearson shuffled papers around his desk. His thin gray hair was combed to the right side to hide the large bald patch on top of his head, obscene amounts of gel caked into the strands and gluing them into place. I stared at a particularly crusty looking spot as he searched for the will my father had put together in this very office.

I wonder if he's ever considered buying a toupee. Or joining the rest of the world in investing in air conditioning so his office feels a little less like the depths of hell.

I could feel sweat trickling down my spine, my sweater clinging to my skin in a way that had me choking back a scream. The room was cramped and stiflingly hot. Dark wooden paneling covering the walls seemed to absorb the light coming in through the window. On the walls behind him, frames holding certificates and degrees hung in neat rows, detailing his accomplishments and awards throughout his career. I rubbed at my nose, fighting the urge to sneeze as I breathed in the musty smell of dust and old books that had mixed with the faint scent of lemon furniture polish.

"Here it is." He cleared his throat, adjusting the thick glasses on his face. "Your father didn't have much, but he did leave you the house and everything in it."

I chewed at the inside of my cheek as I turned my head to stare out the window. I hadn't spoken to my stepfather in nearly six years. Our last conversation ended in a screaming match as I threw garbage bags full of my belongings into the back of my car. Six years without a phone call, a visit, anything. I wouldn't say we'd ever been very close, but the absence of his presence in my life had been a sore spot during milestones and times when a father's guidance would have been welcomed. Mr. Pearson somehow managed to track down my phone number and called me last week to let me know my father had passed and that I needed to come to his office and speak with him as soon as possible. I didn't expect anything, certainly not money, but I was still surprised he'd left me the house.

"Do I have to keep it?" I asked, turning my head to face him. I shifted in my seat, the leather squeaking beneath my weight.

"Uh…no, you don't. You could sell it. I'm not sure what it would go for, but I could help you set up an appraisal if you're interested." He folded his hands on top of the desk, looking at me with a mixture of sympathy and boredom.

I nodded. I didn't want to live there. Those walls held too many memories and I'd rather not sleep surrounded by them. My mom had gotten sick around my thirteenth birthday and declined steadily over the course of the following year. Twelve months and nine days after her diagnosis, we were picking out a casket and a burial plot.

Everything about that house reminded me of her, or rather her absence.

"I do encourage you to at least take a look around. There may be things you'd like to keep or sell, whichever. As far as I know, the property hasn't been touched since your father passed, so all of his belongings should still be in the home." He looked at me expectantly, waiting for me to jump at the opportunity to sift through my father's things, to claim family heirlooms or maybe some prized possession he left behind. There was no sentimentality for me in the objects left in that house, besides my mother's things.

Those I would sort through, maybe I'd take a few things back home with me when I left, but I knew my father. A minimalist, and the least likely man to have left more than a dresser full of clothing and a shelf full of books behind. I stood from the chair, reaching my hand out to shake Mr. Pearson's.

"Thank you for your time. I will call you to set up that appraisal before I head out of town."

"Of course. You have my number if you need help with anything else along the way."

He placed his hand in mine and gave it two firm shakes, pulling back to retrieve the keys from an envelope on top of his desk.

"This key will get you in the front door." He pointed to a long silver key. "This one," he said, holding up a small, ornate key that couldn't fit in anything much bigger than a dollhouse.

"I'm not sure what it goes to. I assume you can figure that out?" The smaller key glinted in the muted light of his office, a glimmer reflecting off the side that made it look like it was glowing. I squinted my eyes at it, trying to find the source of the shimmering light coming from it, when Mr. Pearson cleared his throat. I realized I had leaned in, closer to his outstretched hand, and pulled back quickly. I smoothed the furrow from my brow and attempted a smile.

"Sure thing." I took the keys, slipping them into the pocket of the thick jacket I wore and exited his office, pulling up my hood and sprinting to my car in the downpour of early October rain. From what I remembered, the house was about a twenty minute drive from the office. Settling into my seat, I cranked the heater up and pulled out onto the road.

We're going to get this over with as quickly as possible, and get back home, Cairo. No big deal. It's just a house.

Just a house.

I hadn't ever been particularly close with my stepfather, even before we stopped speaking, though we had just enough of a relationship that the "step" was dropped around a year after he married my mother. He worked a demanding job, meaning he was often absent from dinners and school events. There wasn't any animosity, just a lack of communication that led to a strained relationship as I got older. We both struggled through my teen years. I always felt out of place, no matter where I was. He blamed it on puberty or my mother's passing, but I don't know what it was. Something inside me just never felt comfortable. Everything I did felt hollow, everything I said sounded rehearsed. My friendships were surface-level at best. I had people I sat with at lunch, but I didn't attend their sleepovers or join in on the double dates. After I left Haven, Mississippi, I moved to a bigger city a few hours from home. I did what everyone else around me was doing and went to a small community college, got a somewhat useful degree, and landed a receptionist job at a small accounting office on the outskirts of Tupelo. It had been fine. I made enough money to pay for a one bedroom apartment in a decent area. I had food in my fridge and a car that ran even when it sounded like it was going to fall apart.

That feeling of displacement had stuck with me my entire life, though. I was an outsider, and I wasn't even sure what I was outside of.

A sharp vibration that felt more like a small electric shock pulsed from the pocket of my jacket where the keys sat. I jumped, nearly swerving off the road as I batted at them with my free hand.

Was that static? Maybe the lack of sleep was getting to me. The drive to Haven had been a long one, and I hadn't wanted to shell out any money on a hotel room, so I drove the six hours straight through the night.

I rubbed at my temple with the hand not on the steering wheel. I just needed to get to the house. I'd sort what I could tonight and tomorrow, get some sleep, and go home. I could do this.

CHAPTER 2:
CAIRO

I gave myself a mental pep talk the entire drive, my mind falling silent as I pulled into the gravel driveway of my childhood home. Apart from some obvious signs of aging, it was just as I remembered it.

A two-story white farmhouse with a the wrap-around porch covered in grime from the years it had gone without a good cleaning and a yard in desperate need of maintenance. But the house itself looked so familiar that it made my chest hurt. Memories of my mom chasing me around the living room played through my mind. The smell of sugar cookies wafting through the house as we decorated the Christmas tree, the small dining room where I blew out the candles on the homemade cakes I got every year for my birthday.

A single teardrop rolled slowly over my cheek and down my chin, pulling me out of my thoughts and back into the reality in front of me.

It's just a house, Cairo.

Just a house.

Wiping the wetness from my face, I took a deep breath and stepped out of the car, keeping my head down as I walked up the steps. With each step across the porch, the old wooden boards creaked under my feet. Years of weather and foot traffic had left them warped and discolored in spots.

I fumbled around in my pockets for the keys, pulling them out and slipping the long silver one into the lock and turning it. A familiar click sounded as it turned, the sound resonating in the empty air around me. I pushed against the door, bracing myself against the wave of stale air tinged with the faint scent of lemon Pine-Sol that greeted me as it swung open.

Closing my eyes, I stepped inside and shut the door behind me.

I took a long, steadying breath and opened my eyes to find myself facing the living room, the faded floral-print couch I'd napped on for years sat in the same spot on the worn carpet.

Large canvas prints of our family hung on the walls, the smiles plastered on each of our faces frozen in time. Across the room, the same ancient television sat in the corner. It seemed as if nothing had changed in my absence. I'd left this house six years ago, and it looked just the same now as it had back then, save for the piles of books on the coffee table. Nostalgia washed over me in waves, fueling the ever-growing lump in my throat. I closed my eyes and breathed deeply, inhaling the familiar smells surrounding me. I walked through the room, dragging my fingers across the top of the books and coming away with dust-coated fingertips. Tiny flecks of dust floated in the air, the late afternoon sun streaming in through the bay window on the far side of the room highlighting them as they danced around me.

I wandered deeper into the house, taking my time as I walked through each room and let my mind get reacquainted with the layout of the house.

I found myself at the top of the staircase, standing in front of the door to what used to be my parents' bedroom. The last time I entered this room, my mom was lying in a hospital bed in the center of it. Machines beeped in rhythm with her heart while a tangle of tubes and wires made it impossible to get as close to her as I had wanted to be. I could vividly recall the way the hospice nurse had lifted her frail body, moving her to the far side of the bed to make room for my small frame to crawl in next to her. I fell asleep curled into her side, tear stains streaking my cheeks and soaking the sleeve of her nightgown.

I entered the bedroom, shocked by the lack of furniture and pictures that had once decorated the space. I suppose Dad had moved them all out sometime after I left. The room seemed vulnerable in its bare state, indentions marking the carpet where the bed once sat and the dusty outline of picture frames staining the walls. I walked to the window overlooking the overgrown garden. Weeds that would reach my hips if I stood next to them sprouted from the soil, knotting with each other as they reached for the sky.

My childhood bedroom looked the same as I had left it, posters still clinging to the walls held in place by nail polish-coated thumb tacks. I closed the door on the room and the memories it held and made my way to the door leading to the attic.

A small, abandoned room at the top of the stairs held the missing items from my parents' room. The bed lay in neat pieces in the far corner with photographs and frames and an antique mirror on top of it. I ambled over to a pile of boxes and began sorting through books, carefully wrapped Christmas ornaments, and old baby clothes.

The air in this room was stagnant, the result of having been sealed off for god knows how long. I wondered if my dad had moved all of this up here by himself. The last time I saw him, the years of manual labor had already started taking their toll in the form of a stiff back and perpetually achy joints. Now, thinking of him, the silence throughout the house was deafening. Guilt prodded the back of my mind. I should have been here for him. I knew he was getting older, I knew our time to mend the rift between us was running out. Yet, I stayed away. Why should I reach out if he wasn't going to?

One heart attack later, and any opportunity at a relationship was buried with him.

His funeral had been quick and small. A handful of old co-workers that were still alive trickled in, followed by a few people from his small town that had grown up with him.

He had planned it all himself, no telling how long before he actually passed. But when I got the call that he was gone I was assured the arrangements were taken care of. I just needed to be there within three days for the funeral.

So there I was.

I walked farther back into the room, noticing the heavy layer of dust covering the floor and the massive cobwebs that stretched across the corners where the walls met.

A stack of boxes sat in the back corner of the room captured my attention. I walked toward the smallest one that sat on top and closed my eyes as I forced a deep breath into my lungs.

On the front of the old tattered cardboard was a single word written in faded Sharpie block letters: ALICE

My mom.

CHAPTER 3:

CAIRO

I opened the box, wedging my finger beneath the thick layers of packing tape and pulling it loose. The box opened with a plume of dust, revealing a pile of crumpled newspapers partially covering a small wooden box. I lifted it out, tracing my fingers over the intricate carvings that covered its surface. A keyhole glared at me from the center of the box. I tried leveraging my fingers beneath the clasp and prying it open, but it wouldn't budge. I pulled the keys I'd gotten from Mr. Pearson out of my back pocket, setting aside the house key and plucking the smaller one from my hand. It slid easily into the lock, an odd vibration skittering through my hand as I turned the key and lifted the lid.

Inside, a golden chain lay on top of a black velvet cushion. Pulling it out, I felt a faint recognition at the sight of it. It had a pentagram in the center, a raised silver metal making up the star charm. The golden bevel was faded with age.

I wiped my thumb across its surface, a wave of sadness crashing over me as I held it. I moved to get up when a crinkled envelope caught my eye. I plucked it from the box, pulling out a piece of aged stationary paper and unfolding it to see neat handwriting filling the page.

Alice-

I am writing this letter in the hopes that you will someday be able to come home. I can't imagine what life in Hadeon will look like here without you and Cairo, though I know it is necessary. A certain little boy has locked himself in his room, refusing to come out since he heard the news.

I'm so sorry I couldn't fix this. I'm sorry you have to run. I know the price you will pay, but this necklace belongs with you. You will find it again, when you need it.

I hope when that day comes, the danger to you and Cairo has passed, and you can return to Hadeon.

We will be waiting for you.
Take care of yourselves.
All our love,
Vesper.

I plopped down cross-legged on the floor as I stared at the envelope in my hand. I'd never heard my mom talk about a person named Vesper, though by the sound of the letter I assumed that was intentional. Was Hadeon a town? What could be so dangerous about a town that my mother had kept it a secret from me for my entire life? She'd never talked about her hometown much while I was growing up. From what I knew, she was an only child whose parents died when she was eighteen. She lived in a small town where she attended college, gained her bachelor's degree and my father's last name, and settled down in a little house when they had me. He passed when I was around four years old, too young to actually remember anything about him, and then she married my step-father and we moved in here.

No mysterious town or secret friend or cryptic letters. I set the letter and envelope on the floor in front of me, laying the star of the necklace face up on top of them. Propping my head up with my hand, I stared at the objects at my feet, searching for answers I knew they couldn't give me on their own.

The necklace stirred vague, long forgotten memories of my mother. I grabbed the delicate chain in my hands, gently undoing the clasp and securing it around my neck.

"I hope you don't mind, Mom," I whispered into the empty room.

A gentle static feeling sent goosebumps though my skin where the necklace met my chest. I furrowed my brows as I smoothed my hand over it, and the feeling dissipated.

I stood, brushing the dust from my jeans before tucking the letter and envelope into my back pocket. This had been the longest day I'd had in years. The weight of it settled on my shoulders, causing my eyelids to droop as I entered my old bedroom and sunk down onto the small twin-sized bed. I needed to do some research on the things mentioned in that letter, but I needed to sleep first. In the silence of the empty house, I could hear the light pitter-patter of rain on the tin roof, lulling me into the first deep sleep I'd had in days.

***

I tossed and turned most of the night. Flashes of memories that didn't belong to me crept into my dreams and scrambled my brain as I slept. Images of my mother frantically packing a bag, the panic on her face as she shook my small shoulders and pulled me from my bed. The echo of her words from short snippets of conversations I wasn't privy to were on repeat in my mind as I got up and got dressed for the day.

"We have to go, it isn't safe here anymore."

"He'll find her. He's seen the prophecy."

"I made a deal."

I shook my head, clearing my thoughts and focusing on what I needed to get done that day. It was already nearing noon, and if I planned on being back home on time, I needed to get busy.

I pulled a sweater over my head and buttoned the blue jeans I'd put on. There wasn't much to do for my hair, as the mass of dark curls was now a tangled nest after such a fitful sleep. I pushed open the door to the small bathroom attached to my room and checked the damage in the mirror. Yup. I could definitely house a handful of birds in that bitch. I combed my fingers through it the best I could and tossed it in a ponytail that hung low on my head. There were dark circles under my eyes, the purple-ish hue making my gray eyes appear dull in the fluorescent light of the bathroom. I splashed water on my face and let out a long breath.

Okay. To-do list.

I needed to get my room cleared out, then start on the rest of the house, box up what I wanted to keep, and label what could be sold. I rubbed at my brow, realizing the magnitude of the job before me.

Speaking of jobs, I had only taken two days off from work to go to take care of this.

This was going to take more than two days. A sweat broke out along my forehead, anxiety building at the overwhelming task ahead of me.

I reached for the necklace I wore, rubbing the charm that rested just below my collarbone with my fingers. A sudden need to find out more about the letter I found upstairs swarmed through me. Who wrote it? Why was it hidden? My mom had been my best friend. We told each other everything right up until the day she passed, so why would she keep this from me? What danger was the person in the letter talking about?

Maybe it was an excuse to put off taking care of the house, but my mind was focused solely on figuring out what she was hiding.

I wanted answers. No, I *needed* them. The need was a living breathing thing crawling under my skin. I clutched the necklace tighter in my palm, feeling my heart rate accelerate.

"Hadeon." The world rolled off my tongue like an incantation, my fingers drumming against my leg in anticipation.

I felt a pull, a draw somewhere in my chest to go. I almost felt…home-sick. Out of nowhere, I desperately needed to be there.

Now.

I didn't give myself time to think it through. Instead, I rushed back into my room, tossing my clothes from yesterday back into my duffle and slinging it over my shoulder. I made it downstairs and into my car before I regained any logic. I didn't know where it was. I pulled out my phone, bringing up the GPS and typing in Hadeon.

Nothing.

A quick google search gave me the same result. I huffed in frustration, my leg bouncing in rhythm with my accelerated heartbeat.

Okay, we'll figure it out. Just think.

I pulled my duffle into my lap from the back seat and rifled through until I found the letter again.

I scanned it for any useful information, flipping it over to check the back before exhaling dramatically and tossing it in the seat next to me.

I propped my head in my hand, steadily drumming my fingers on the steering wheel as I thought. Early morning sunlight broke through the clouds above me, shining warm sunbeams through the windshield where they hit the envelope and letter in the passenger seat. I glanced over, squinting at the envelope in the sunlight. The way the light hit it, I could see a faint script print in the top left hand corner of the faded paper.

Stationary. It was personalized stationary, with an address on it.

The print was faded, but I could just barely make out what the last line said.
    Hadeon, LA.
    Louisiana, here I come.

WHAT LIES BETWEEN US

CHAPTER 4:
CAIRO

The road stretched on through miles of empty fields and small run-down towns. The direction alerts from the GPS were the only sounds in the car other than my nails tapping anxiously along the steering wheel as I drove, in a constant battle to convince myself I wasn't insane for following a whim to a state I'd never been to. I was nearly four hours into the drive, the restlessness from being in my car for so long only adding to the growing anxiety over my decision to make this trip in the first place. From the moment I clasped my mom's necklace around my neck, I felt it settle deep inside my chest. A pulling, nagging feeling that guided me to Louisiana and despite the logical side of my brain knowing that it should be impossible, I knew it would guide me the rest of the way to Hadeon.

An uneasiness had cloaked my body in the middle of the night, and since waking from that nightmare I couldn't think about anything other than the town my mother came from, that I came from. Why had she hidden it from me? Why had she never mentioned it? Either way, I didn't think I could turn the car around and drive away if I wanted to—the pull in my chest was too strong and too insistent. There was something in that town that I needed to see, or do, or know.

The cool metal of the necklace was an unfamiliar but comforting weight against my skin as I drove, keeping my mind grounded as the hours dwindled down. My phone chimed, alerting me that I was fourteen miles from my destination. I breathed deeply through my nose, scanning the exit signs for something that would tell me where I was actually going, just as a low hum began to build inside the car.

"What the hell?" I checked the gauges on my dash, made sure none of the lights were on, shut off the air conditioner, and made sure all the windows were rolled up as the sound grew louder. My heartbeat became erratic as the necklace began to warm against my skin, a subtle heat spreading through my body like a pulse. I touched my fingers to it, hoping I'd imaged the sensation, but the shock of warm metal under my fingertips nearly caused me to swerve off the road. The humming leveled out into a rhythmic *thump thump thump*, like a heartbeat. Up ahead a green exit sign caught my eye, no obvious town to claim it, just a solid green sign with an arrow pointing to the gravel road off the side of the highway. A flutter of light blinked rapidly over the sign like a beacon, calling me to follow it. I gritted my teeth and flipped my turn signal on, veering toward the exit. My phone screen flickered, the GPS faltering and disconnecting as I turned off the main road. I dragged a hand through my hair, questioning my sanity and the instincts I'd followed thus far. The road narrowed into a single lane winding through a dense forest and then shifted into gravel. My tires crunched over it as I drove, a rough sound that echoed around the silent car. The sun had begun setting rapidly in the last few minutes, the bright rays of sunshine dimming as they fell behind the trees and disappeared altogether.

"What am I even doing?" I asked the empty air around me. I was not a spontaneous person. I liked order, organization, and planning. I didn't just jump into the car and drive to a different state on a whim because of a "feeling." I felt the necklace warm further at my turmoil, almost as if it were comforting me, encouraging me to keep going. Part of me still thought I was losing my mind, but the other part knew that there was an undeniable guidance coming from around my neck. Maybe it was my mother. The thought was comforting in my chaotic state of mind.

I followed the winding curves of the gravel road, every bump jostling my body and my nerves as I pleaded with my sanity to stick around for a little bit longer.

I drove under a canopy of tree branches that had stretched out toward the road, intertwining with each other and creating a tunnel of leaves, spotlights shining through as the sun fought its way between the dense foliage. The area on the other side of the canopy seemed to shimmer, like a heatwave rising from hot asphalt, except there wasn't enough heat here to create that effect. The moment my bumper met the start of it, I felt a subtle resistance. It felt like the air around me thickened for just a split second as I pushed down on the accelerator and forced the car to move forward. My ears popped, a tingling sensation skittering over my skin as my eyesight waned for a single heartbeat and then cleared. I shook my head, my hands clenching on the steering wheel as my heart galloped in my chest. I urged myself to keep going, to not stop and analyze every odd occurrence I'd experienced in the last day. My car kept trudging along, taking another turn and cresting a little hill.

A small wooden structure came into view. Composed of moss-riddled, aged wood and standing about four feet high on the right side of the road, a wooden post with a sign hanging from it read "Welcome to Hadeon."

Hadeon.

I'd found it.

Well, the necklace had found it. I'd pretty much been dragged here by sheer stupidity and intuition. Either way, I'd made it.

Exhaustion hummed under my skin as I passed the sign, my car bumping along the gravel road until it smoothed out into cobblestone. Large stone buildings and small cottages lined the street on either side of me. The worn exteriors felt inviting as I swiveled my head left and right, taking in the quaint beauty of the town. Tall lampposts dotted every corner, the illusion of being lit by candles instead of bulbs making them feel cozy and magical. A neon motel sign caught my attention farther down the road. The building was long and made of mismatched stones, giving it an almost haphazard charm. I pulled into the parking lot, my headlights illuminating the front office.

"Mordell Motel," I read the sign aloud. Well, I hope Mordell has a room available. Fatigue started creeping in about halfway through the trip, and the strange incidents that had happened since then had given me short jolts of adrenaline that only ended up adding to my weariness as they wore off. I grabbed my duffel out of the back seat, casting a glance over my shoulder as I did. The street was empty, but an unsettling stillness hung in the air, a thickness that lingered in the atmosphere around me like fog. I shrugged the feeling off, chalking it up to my overtired state, and trudged inside the front office. My eyes widened as I froze mid-step and took in the…eclectic decor. Frogs. There were frogs fucking *everywhere*. The wallpaper looked like mottled green skin. Shelves lining the walls were crammed with figurines, stuffed toys, paintings, and framed pictures.

All of them were frogs.

"Don't you love them?" a voice chirped, startling me. I spun around to find a lanky man behind the counter, a wide grin splitting his face. His uniform resembled something you'd see in a 1950s style movie, complete with the odd little bellhop hat perched slightly askew on his head.

"It was certainly a choice," I said.

He beamed at me. "Designed it myself!"

I stared blankly back at him. What was I supposed to say to that? If I didn't compliment the man's frogs, was he going to eat me or something? I didn't have time to formulate a response that I thought would be acceptable to the odd man because he just kept talking.

"Welcome to the Mordell Motel. I'm Tim, how may I be of service tonight?" He clapped his hands together with an energy that was borderline manic, clasping them together and resting them under his chin as he stared at me.

"I just need a room," I replied, too tired to do more than blink at him.

"EXCELLENT!" he practically shouted.

"Yes." I blinked at him again, unsure why this required so much enthusiasm.

"Good, good, good," he murmured to himself, his fingers flying over the keyboard in front of him.

"Well you are in luck, milady." He tipped an imaginary hat, which was odd, considering he had a very real hat currently sitting on his head. "I have a vacant suite with your name on it."

I scribbled my name into his guestbook and took the key he offered, mumbling a half-hearted thank you. As I headed out of the office and toward the outdoor walkway that led to the rooms, I could feel his eyes on me, unblinking.

Note to self: use all available locks on the door tonight.

The hallway leading to the suite was narrow and dimly lit, a cool breeze coming in from each open end. Vintage sconces threw out shadows that danced along the walls as I walked. Halfway down, a set of old vending machines stood recessed into an alcove. The machines buzzed faintly, their outdated design boasting faded logos for soda brands I hadn't seen in years.

I took a step closer to them before I noticed the crow perched on top of the machine farthest from me. Its glossy black feathers shimmered in the dim light, beady eyes locked on mine, unblinking and far too intelligent.

Goosebumps erupted across my skin as I watched the bird cock its head to the side, small black eyes gleaming in the low light as it studied me.

"Hello, bird," I muttered under my breath, keeping my eye on it as I fed dollar bills into the machine and grabbed a snack. *Lovely, I'm talking to birds now.*

The crow tilted its head again, and let out a low caw that echoed down the empty hallway. I hurried past, shoving the key into the door of the suite and stepping inside, resisting the urge to look back and see if it had decided to follow me.

I winced as I flipped the light switch, expecting a room devoted to alligators or snakes, but a sigh of relief escaped my mouth when I glanced around the room and found bland beige walls, simple white linens, and a distinct lack of amphibious decor.

Shrugging out of my clothes, I dug through my bag until I found an oversized sleep shirt and shrugged it on. I managed to wash my face, slapping aimlessly at the light switch on my way to the bed, and then collapsed in a boneless heap of exhaustion.

Outside, the sound of fluttering wings disturbed the quiet, faint but unmistakable. I froze, but a second later the noise was gone.

Everything I needed to figure out could wait until tomorrow. I rolled onto my side, my fingers finding the charm hanging around my neck. I rubbed it's surface, the motion soothing me as my eyes drifted shut.

CHAPTER 5:

CAIRO

Thunder *rattles the ground beneath my feet as I stand in a small kitchen, looking out into the backyard that grows darker by the second. The oak tree at the back of the property has become a swirling mass of leaves in the wind, branches thrashing through the air like they're trying to break free. A bolt of fear pierces my heart, forcing it into a gallop as I drop the soapy sponge in my hand and run to the back door and out into the storm.*

"CAIRO!" I scream. Under the oak tree I see the vague outlines of two small bodies, huddled together as they kneel in the dirt. My pulse hammers as I race toward them on shaking legs. A bolt of lightning cracks the sky, touching down just outside of our yard and shattering a portion of the fence. I throw a hand over my eyes to shield them from the flash of light.

"CAIRO COME HERE!" My words are so loud they burn my throat as they come up, but they are carried away by the wind of the storm before they reach her little ears.

I'm close, I will make it to her. Just a few more yards. I push my legs faster, my arms pumping at my sides even through the fire that races through my lungs at the exertion. Another bolt of lightning descends, crashing into the ground just a few feet in front of me and tossing me backward. My back hits the ground, and all of the air inside me leaves in a painful whoosh.

"Mama?" Cairo calls to me, her voice small and sure as ever, even in the face of the storm surrounding us.

I push myself up, standing and bending to catch my breath as she makes her way to me, her hand wrapped in the slightly larger one of the boy walking next to her.

"You two have to come inside, right now." I reach my hands out to them, the rain pelting them with water so cold I'm surprised it hasn't turned to ice.

"It's okay, Mama. She said it's okay." The two of them turn back toward the tree and the gap in the fence where the lightning shattered the wood. Cairo turns, pulling on the hand of the boy next to her.

"Cairo, STOP!" A sense of dread leaches into my veins, spreading through my body like a fast moving poison and piercing my heart. They keep moving, their pace steady as they walk through the wind and rain without wavering. Cairo turns to look at me over her shoulder.

"It's okay, Mama. She knows who I am. She says she chose me."

I take off in a full run toward them, but the wind pushing back against my body makes it feel like I'm running through mud as my arms pump at my sides.

"Baby, come here! Come to mama!" My words never reach them. My feet sink into the mud. I lose my balance and hit my knees with a crack, the sound of the children's giggles washing over me. A gust of wind sweeps my hair over my eyes, temporarily blinding me before I shove it back with dirty hands.

And then, they are gone.

Only two sets of muddy footprints leading to the edge of the yard, and not a trace of my baby.

"CAIRO!" I scream and scream, my voice cracking and breaking each time her name leaves my lips. The wind around me settles, the storm clouds receding and allowing the stars overhead to shine through the darkness that surrounds me. My hands shake as I lift them to wipe the tear stains from my face.

I fall to my back in the dirt, closing my eyes as the world around me goes silent. A heaviness settles over my body like fog. My limbs like lead, my breaths deep and even.

Was I sleeping?

"Cairo."

"Cairo." An urgent whisper trickled down to me through the thick layer of fog that had settled over my brain, a note of desperation clinging to the syllables in my name.

"CAIRO." The voice snapped, ripping me from my sleep and hurtling me into the dark reality of the motel room. My eyes shot open, locking onto the dark ceiling above me while my pulse hammered. I sat straight up in bed, the blanket falling to my waist as I peered into the dark for the voice that startled me awake.

"Cairo. Get up, we have to go," a deep voice hissed. The lamp on the nightstand flicked on, illuminating the man beside my bed. He stood in front of me, his hand outstretched as he reached toward me. I'd never been in a fight, but instincts are a hell of a thing.

A scream ripped from my throat as I swung my fist around, connecting with the intruder's throat, jerking my arm back as he stumbled backward.

"What th-JESUS CHRIST," he wheezed with his hands clutched to his neck as I scrambled off the bed and across the room to the door. I turned the knob just as two large hands slammed against it from either side of me. Panic took root deep in my gut, a primal sense of fight or flight. I kicked my leg back as hard as I could, clipping him in the shin before he hopped out of the way, coughing as he kept his hands braced against the door.

"Fuck, Cairo, relax for a goddamn second." His voice was raspy, and close enough to my ear to send warning chills down my spine. I held my breath, my hands clammy on the doorknob as I felt him pull back and lift a hand from the door.

He reached over and flipped on the light switch, taking a single step back and giving me space to turn around.

"I'm not going to hurt you," he whispered softly. "I just need you to listen to me for a second, please." I could hear my blood pounding in my ears. What choice did I have? If he was a serial killer he was a really odd one. He seemed panicked, a hefty amount of urgency in his tone as he spoke. He was almost desperate. Pleading.

I moved slowly, painfully aware of the fact that I was braless, unarmed, and this man knew my name. I turned fully to face him, my eyes trailing from the black boots at his feet, up his long blue jean-clad legs, to the thick black hoodie he was wearing. Raising my head, my eyes stuttered over his neck. The red mark where I punched him was one of the few areas not covered in swirling black tattoos. He reached out one of his large hands, slowly, as if he were approaching a wild animal, and rested one finger under my chin, raising my eyes to meet his.

Green.

So green.

Not green like grass, or emeralds, but green like a cat. Like an apple, or the glistening flesh of a lime. Flashes of something from my childhood flitted behind my eyes, but I couldn't catch any of the images to examine them further. Small snippets of a young boy with messy black hair and glowing green eyes, a weathered hand slipping me a piece of candy wrapped in a gold foil.

"Cairo, we need to leave." He rested his hands gently on my shoulders as he spoke.

I took a step back, a brow raised as I crossed my arms over my chest. "Leave?" I echoed. "Who even are you?"

What kind of deranged ape bursts into someone's room and tries to get them to agree to their own kidnapping? A sad smile lifted the side of his mouth.

"Think, Cai. Think really hard."

My brows knitted together at his words.

Cai.

No one called me that, no one…except…

The boy with the green eyes and unruly black hair…

There was no way. It wasn't just impossible, it was batshit fucking insane to even entertain it.

"What is my name?" he pleaded.

"I-I don't know."

"Yes, you do. I can see it all over your face." He turned his back to me, pacing a small circle while he scrubbed his hands over his face in frustration.

"Don't punch me again, okay?" he said in a hushed tone as he walked toward me, pushing up the sleeve of his jacket. Reaching for my hand he pressed my fingertips against his wrist and held them there.

"What are you doing?"

"Feel it."

I carefully moved my fingers in a small circle, feeling the raised edges of a scar. He held his wrist closer to me as I examined it with my eyes. A star. A star-shaped scar, dead center on his wrist. Invisible unless you're

31

looking for it or feeling it thanks to the faded white color and the myriad of tattoos surrounding it.

My heart thumped heavily in my chest.

I've known one person in my life with a scar like that. Just one.

"What. Is. My. Name?" he asked again. His eyes bounced between mine, a desperate determination evident in them as he waited for me to say the name I hadn't thought about in years.

"Radley…"

CHAPTER 6:
CAIRO

H e blew a deep breath out of his nose, his shoulders lowering with relief as he spoke.

"Good to know you haven't completely forgotten me then." He let out a dry chuckle.

"I don't understand. How are you——"

"I will explain, I promise, but we really need to leave. You shouldn't have come here." He walked over to the dresser and wrenched a drawer open, grabbing the few stacks of clothes I had in there and piling them on the bed.

"Where is your luggage?" Quick steps carried him across the room where he snatched my jacket off the top of the dresser and tossed it at me.

"It's under the bed." A wave of dizzying nausea made my throat feel tight. I couldn't make sense of what I was seeing in front of me.

He grabbed it and began tossing everything inside. The book and makeup bag on my nightstand, the clothes I had stripped off before I passed out—everything I brought was being unceremoniously thrown into a single duffle bag. He threw a pair of sweatpants in my direction and turned around while I shrugged them on in a daze, my mind trying its hardest to make sense of what was happening.

Radley wasn't a real person. He was my imaginary friend. The last time I'd seen him I was eight. The night after my eighth birthday we hid under the blanket on top of the small single bed I used to sleep on and told each other scary stories, a flashlight and a bowl of popcorn and hours of shrieking and laughing from the stories we came up with. The next morning my mom and I left. I never found out why and I never saw Radley again.

Months went by, during which I screamed and begged my mom to let me see him, only to be told he never existed at all. I saw multiple therapists that all told me the same thing.

Radley didn't exist.

I had made him up, and at some point, my brain decided it didn't need him anymore. Yet, here he was. Alive, aged by more than a decade, and standing right in front of me.

"Get your keys. I'll drive." Radley's voice broke me out of the trance I'd fallen in, and I forced my legs to carry me to where my purse sat on top of the small table by the motel door. Pulling my keys out of the inside pocket, I held them out, still dazed as Radley took them from my hand and ushered me out of the room with my duffle slung over his shoulder and his hand on the small of my back.

"Cai?" His voice was so much deeper than the last time I'd heard it. The voice of a fully grown man.

"I'm going to drive past the town line, and then I'm going to get out of the car and you are going to drive away. Do you understand?"

No. No, I didn't understand. But, Jesus. How was he here? Was I going to risk him being an axe murderer to find out?

Yup.

"Fine. You have until then to tell me what the hell is going on, Radley." I pushed past him, folding myself into the passenger side of the car and slamming the door shut a little harder than necessary. Radley tossed my bag in the back seat before getting in the car and starting the engine. He reached over to brace his hand against my headrest, looking back over his shoulder as he backed out of the parking lot.

"I don't know how much to tell you. I don't know how much you'll believe," he sighed.

The car rolled backward as he shifted from reverse to drive and pulled out onto the empty road.

"Right now, neither do I."

He glanced at me, shaking his head as he looked back at the road in front of us.

"Cai…"

"You aren't real," I murmured.

"What?" He choked out a laugh, turning his head to give me an amused look.

"You aren't real. You're my imaginary friend." I leaned my head against the window.

"Jesus. Is that what she told you?" He sounded angry, offended by that statement.

As I opened my mouth to respond, the radio turned on, blaring at full volume. I smacked my hands over my ears, screaming in surprise as the windshield wipers turned on. In the next minute both of our seatbelts came unlatched and the headlights flickered out, leaving us hurtling down the road in complete darkness. Radley cursed under his breath, pulling over and jerking the car into park just in front of the "Welcome to Hadeon" sign.

"We're going to have to walk." He got out, slamming the car door shut and retrieving my bag from the back seat.

"Walk where?" I asked, getting out and sprinting to catch up to him. "Radley, stop! You have to explain what the hell is going on. Why can't I stay? And how are you even here right now?" I yelled as thunder cracked in the distance. Rain began to fall around us, plastering my hair to my forehead and forcing me to squint to see Radley's figure moving at a brisk pace down the road.

"I don't have time!" he roared back. He stopped dead in his tracks, spinning to face me. "You shouldn't be here, Cairo. How did you even find this place?" God, he looked so angry. His eyebrows were drawn low over his eyes, his mouth set in a tight line as he glared at me.

"It's a town, it wasn't that hard to find." I decided to leave out the part about my mom's necklace practically dragging me here. I still hadn't had time to fully accept that and I had a feeling it wouldn't make him any happier anyway.

He let out a dry chuckle.

"Just a town." He shook his head back and forth, sending water droplets flying. He locked his hands behind his neck and tilted his head to the sky, his eyes closed in what looked like a prayer. I stood there in the middle of the street, the rain soaking through the sweatshirt I'd thrown on and causing a deep chill to seep under my skin. The wind whipped around us as the storm picked up strength. The only light this close to the edge of town came from the glimpses of the moon as it peaked out behind the darkening clouds to glimpse the train wreck happening below.

Radley blew out a hard breath and stormed over to me.

"Cairo, how did you find out about this town?"

"I found a letter. A letter and a necklace, and they both kind of... lead me here," I mumbled the last part, not wanting him to think I was completely insane.

"A letter from who?"

"I don't know. Someone named Vesper, but I don't know who they are."

His eyes flew wide, his jaw tight as he rubbed his hand over his mouth. "Vesper. Of course."

"My turn. Why exactly am I not supposed to be here?"

Radley looked down the road that lead out of town and back to me, his entire body tensing as thunder rumbled around us again.

"I can't explain everything right now. Not here." He cursed under his breath, pulling out his phone and firing off a text before shoving it back into his pocket.

"We're going to leave your car here for now. I'll have someone take it to my house. We can't walk in this weather and that," he gestured at my car, "definitely isn't getting us anywhere right now."

"So, I'm going to your house?" Nerves swarmed my stomach. A part of me, buried somewhere deep inside, recognized the man in front of me. A smaller version of him, of course, but it was still him. The rest of me was sifting through every crime show I'd ever seen and sounding alarms in my mind. How stupid would it be to go with him?

But what choice did I really have? I had questions and he had the answers. I didn't come all this way just to turn back around now.

He looked torn as he studied me.

"Yes. As much as I would love to get you back across that town line, it's not possible."

The words came out through gritted teeth. He walked back to my car and leaned against the hood, crossing his arms over his broad chest and hanging his head toward the ground.

I shifted my weight from foot to foot. He seemed to be different from the Radley that begged me to remember his name not thirty minutes ago.

The lines of his body were rigid, his jaw locked tight as he stared anywhere but at me.

I hadn't encountered a single thing today that made any sense, and this was just the cherry on top. Why wasn't I supposed to be here? What did he know that I didn't? I wasn't even going to touch the not-able-to-leave-town thing. It was too much already. My nerves were shot, my head was pounding, and I desperately wanted to take a shower and a nap.

The next crack of thunder echoed around us, bringing with it a fresh downpour of rain that fell in fat drops at my feet.

"Shit. Come here." Radley pushed off the car, opening the passenger door and beckoning me to get inside. I obliged, folding myself into the seat and wiping at the rain splattered on my face with the sleeve of my shirt. The driver side door opened and Radley crawled in. The silence in the car was only made bearable by the sounds of the storm brewing on the other side of the windshield.

I felt like my entire life had been flipped upside down. There were obvious secrets hiding in my past, things my mother purposefully kept from me, and with her gone I had to find the answers myself. Then there was Radley. The harder I tried to make sense of the man in front of me, the more my brain felt like hot mud. How was he here? Why was he so upset that I was? Confusion and exhaustion bubbled in the back of my head in the form of a headache.

"I'm sorry." His voice broke through my thoughts, wrenching my attention back to him.

"Sorry for what?"

"Everything. Scaring you earlier, being a dick to you now, the entire situation we're in." He leaned his head back against the headrest and shut his eyes.

"There's so much I need to explain to you, Cairo." His eyes opened, locking onto mine. "I just need you to keep an open mind when I do, okay?"

CHAPTER 7:

CAIRO

The minutes ticked by in silence. I could almost feel the agitation rolling off of Radley in waves as he sat in the driver's seat, his hands tightening and relaxing on the wheel in a repetitive motion.

"You good over there?" I asked. The tension in the car had become palpable and I was suffocating in it. What good was an open mind if he wasn't going to explain anything?

"I'm just trying to understand how this happened."

"Yeah, you and me both," I said under my breath.

Headlights appeared in the rearview mirror, cutting through the wall of rain cloaking the road.

The car pulled over behind us as Radley got out.

"That's Jax. Come on."

I pushed my hair back on my face and took a deep breath.

I wasn't going to get murdered.

I was going to get answers.

I followed Radley to the car, bypassing the passenger door he held open and sliding in the back instead. He shook his head with a huff.

No way in hell I was sitting up there with yet another man I didn't know.

In the driver's seat was a tall, tan-skinned man that looked to be around our age. His brown hair was trimmed into a buzz cut and I noticed a prominent scar that bisected his eyebrow as he turned to look at me.

"Picking up strays, Radley?" he asked, his gaze still roaming over me.

"Just shut up and drive."

"Touchy tonight." He chuckled, putting the car in reverse and backing up onto the road, heading back into town.

The silence stretched on as we passed streetlamps and darkened shops. The town was dead this late at night with only the fading sounds of the storm outside to help alleviate the stifling awkwardness inside this car.

Jax cleared his throat, his eyes darting to the rear view mirror as he spoke.

"So, you have a name?"

"Cairo," I mumbled.

His head snapped to Radley's so fast I anticipated the sound of his neck bone breaking.

"What the fuck?"

"Can you keep your eyes on the road? I've got it under control."

"So, you've heard of me then?" I asked Jax. My head turned toward Radley. "And you, you have what under control, exactly?" I leaned forward in my seat, resting an arm on the back of each of their chairs. I wasn't a thing to have under control. And I still wasn't sure why I wasn't supposed to be here.

Jax let out a low whistle.

"Got your work cut out for you there, buddy."

The house finally came into view and I just barely held in my gasp.

Looming before us was a towering Victorian-style home, hundreds of years old by the looks of it, and painted jet-black. The shutters, the porch, the spindles on the railings—all black.

If Dracula lived in the south, this is the home he would live in.

"Good lord," I whispered.

Jax rolled his eyes.

"Yeah, yeah. We're all impressed with Money Bags here."

The car rolled to a stop in front of the house, and Radley immediately got out and opened my door.

"You're welcome!" Jax yelled from his seat.

Radley handed me my bag and a key ring from his pocket, sorting through them until he landed on the one he was looking for and handed it to me.

"Go on inside, I'll be there in just a minute."

"Okay." I took the key from his outstretched hand and walked to the front door, my eyes roving over the dozens of different plants and flowers that lined the walkway to the porch. Small lanterns hung from stakes in between them, illuminating the path. I turned the key in the lock, entering the foyer and closing the door behind me.

My jaw dropped.

This was where he lived?

It seemed so...opulent.

Rich wood covered the walls, contrasting the black-and-white checkered marble floors beneath my feet. A black chandelier hung above my head, casting prisms of light across the small room. It was beautiful. Decadent.

The door opened and slammed behind me, and I turned to see Radley shaking his hair out behind me as he toed off the heavy black boots he wore.

"Sorry about that." He reached behind him, grabbing the fabric of his hoodie and pulling it over his head. The thin white t-shirt he wore underneath it rose with the motion, displaying a sliver of a toned, tan abdomen, causing heat to flare in my cheeks. I turned my head away, busying myself with tying my hair up while he slung the jacket over a coat rack behind the door.

"I've got a couple guest rooms upstairs, only one has an attached bathroom though, so you might be most comfortable in there."

"Lead the way."

I followed him up the winding staircase, the view of the foyer from this angle making it look even larger.

He stopped at a door at the end of the hallway, pushing it open and flicking on the light switch.

I entered the room behind him, setting my duffle on the massive bed that sat against the back wall.

"The bathroom is just through there." He pointed at an open doorway to the left of the room, then to the one directly across from it. "That one is the closet."

"Thank you," I uttered quietly.

"I know you have questions, Cairo. I promise I'll answer them. Take a shower and get comfortable. I'll get us something to drink and be back in a bit, okay?"

"Yeah, sounds good." I plopped down on the bed, running my hand over the embroidered design on the comforter.

"So I guess this means you aren't my long-lost imaginary friend?" I joked, watching his back as he walked toward the door.

He turned his head to look at me over his shoulder.

"No. Not imaginary, Cai." He shook his head, his eyes meeting the floor rather than my own. "Just lost."

And then he left.

CHAPTER 8:

CAIRO

Radley came back into the room an hour later. I was sitting on the bed, freshly showered, carefully running a Wet Brush through my curls when he knocked on the door.

"Come in," I said, just loud enough for him to hear me.

He opened the door, balancing a tray in one hand.

"I brought some tea. I wasn't sure if you'd feel up to eating or not, but I grabbed some snacks too just in case."

A steaming cup of tea sat on the tray next to a plate of various cheeses and fruits, all carefully arranged in a circle. He perched on the edge of the bed, setting the tray on top of the comforter next to him.

"Oh. Thank you." The man made me a charcuterie board? After the way he acted in the car, and the middle of the road after that, his doting demeanor now was a little jarring.

"Look, I know I was an ass earlier."

"You were," I agreed. His eyebrows raised as he looked at me.

"You didn't think I'd agree? In the last twenty-four hours I've had the most horrific, vivid nightmares I've ever experienced. I've driven aimlessly to a place I've never heard of, only to be woken up by someone I didn't think existed, who then told me I wasn't supposed to be here. I don't have the energy to placate you."

"That's fair." He blew out a breath, combing his fingers through the roots of his damp hair. "Alright, where do you want me to start?"

"I guess...why were you trying to get me out of town?"

He drummed his fingers along his leg as he thought of a response.

"It's dangerous, Cairo. There are reasons why you and your mom left in the first place."

"Reasons like what?"

"I don't know, not for sure. I just know what I was told."

"Which was?"

"That you were both in danger, and that you couldn't ever come back."

"Danger from who?"

"I don't know that either, I'm sorry."

I finished smoothing out the tangles in my hair and set the comb down on the nightstand beside the bed.

"And now that I'm here, I can't leave?" Leaning back against the headboard, I folded my arms across my stomach. My eyes were already growing heavy, despite my need for answers.

"Correct." The words came out like they pained him to say. Each syllable sounding like sandpaper in his mouth.

"And that is due to…magic?" I didn't mean for the word to come out dripping in doubt, but it did. Radley just smiled, the corners of his full lips tilting just slightly to match the amusement dancing in his eyes.

"Yes, but that is going to have to be a much longer conversation."

I nodded. What else was I going to say? Enough weird shit had happened lately that I couldn't exactly rule it out. The reality of the situation made my stomach drop. I was trapped here. It's not like I had an incredibly fulfilling life to go back to, but there were bound to be people that noticed my absence. My boss, Mr. Pearson, maybe.

"So…nice mansion you have here." I regretted the words as soon as I said them, but what was a guy my age doing living in a fucking McMansion? I was too curious not to bring it up.

"It was my parents' house. After my dad passed, my mom couldn't stay here, but she couldn't let it go either. I stayed and she moved to a smaller place in town. Jax stays here a lot too, so it worked out." He shrugged, the slight blush in his cheeks telling me he was aware of the price tag a place like this carried.

I nodded, picking at a loose thread on the comforter before saying what I needed to.

"I can't just stay here, Radley. I have a life outside of this place." A pretty pitiful one, but he didn't need to know that, and regardless, I had to go back sometime.

"I will help you figure this out, okay? We'll do whatever it takes."

I could see the determination in his face. Whether it was because I really was in danger, or because he didn't want me here for other reasons, he would help me find a way out. I knew that much.

I took a long sip of my tea, letting the warm liquid heat me from the inside out and chase away the chill this new information had given me. Setting the cup back on the tray, I forced my eyes to meet his.

"Who is Vesper?"

His jaw ticked, and he rubbed a hand over it before he answered. "My mother."

This time it was my eyebrows that shot up to my hairline.

"So our moms, they were—"

"Best friends. All their lives from what I've gathered."

"I don't understand how I don't remember this place. I don't remember ever living anywhere except Haven, I just remember you. Even those memories are faded though."

"Cairo, there is something important I need to tell you before you go searching for any more answers from anyone else in this place."

"Okay."

"They don't—the people in this town, no one remembers you. No one remembers either of you."

My brow furrowed. How? What happened to erase us after we left? For what purpose?

"I can take you to see her, if you want. Then you can see it for yourself."

"Yes, please." I was desperate for answers, for a connection to my mother. I wanted to see where we had lived, I wanted to trace my hands along the walls of the room I played in as a child in hopes that it would stir buried memories and help me remember this world.

"We'll go in the morning. For now, just try to get some rest. I'm just across the hall, if you need anything."

"Thank you, Radley."

"You're welcome. Sweet dreams, Cai."

The door closed with a soft click as Radley left the room, leaving me with my sleep-addled mind spinning.

So I was stuck.

Breathe, Cairo.

That was fine. I wasn't going to freak out.

In, out. In, out.

I definitely wasn't going to have a panic attack over it or anything dramatic like that.

Holy fuck, my lungs are on fire.

The walls were decidedly not closing in on me.

Ohmygod. Ohmygod. Ohmygod.

I was good. Super good. I was—

Going to throw up.

I threw back the comforter, bolting for the toilet and made it just in time to see the measly vending machine lunch I'd scarfed down after checking in at the motel come back up.

Okay. Not ideal, but not the end of the world. I stood, moving to the counter and rifling through the drawers until I found a new toothbrush still in the package.

After scrubbing the aftertaste of bile out of my mouth, I climbed back into the bed, counting down from one hundred over and over until my mind gave up and let me win the fight for sleep.

CHAPTER 9:

CAIRO

The smell of coffee lured me out of bed the next morning, the house quiet aside from the faint sounds of clanging metal and muffled curses coming from the kitchen as I came down the stairs. I pushed open the double doors, stifling a laugh at the picture before me.

Radley stood with a smoking pan in one hand and a dish towel in the other, furiously fanning the remnants of what I guessed were pancakes, a constant stream of curses coming from his mouth as he used his elbow to turn on the faucet and threw the pan in the sink.

A loud sizzle sounded just minutes before the smoke alarm did.

"Oh fuck me." He slapped his hands down on the counter, using them to push himself up until he stood on top of it, and reached for the smoke detector on the ceiling. He pulled the entire thing down, chucking it into the sink along with the pan.

I slapped a hand over my mouth, forcing the laughter to stay firmly inside as I watched him flail around the room.

He turned toward me at the sound, propping his hands on his hips and letting his head hang down as he exhaled.

"Not a word," he muttered.

I put my hands up in surrender.

"I wasn't going to say a thing." I tried and failed to keep the amusement out of my voice. Radley dismounted from the counter and stood in front of the various bowls and utensils spread out across its surface.

"How do you feel about going out for breakfast? It's a good excuse to stop by my mom's house."

"Works for me." I lifted one shoulder in a shrug.

Radley scrubbed at his hands before gathering his phone and wallet from his room and meeting me back downstairs where I followed him through the kitchen into an attached garage. A black SUV was parked next to a small motorcycle.

"Got a preference?" he asked.

"Not really." I shook my head. I hadn't been on a bike before, but I wasn't against it.

"Bike it is," he said with a smirk as he walked to a shelf against the far wall, pulling two helmets down and handing one to me.

"Safety first." He winked at me and hung his helmet on the handlebars, then held his palm outstretched toward me.

"Do you have a hair tie?"

I slid the elastic band off my wrist and held it out in front of us with a raised eyebrow.

I stood rigid as he walked behind me and gathered my hair, pulling it toward him and quickly braiding the mass together before securing it with the hair tie.

That's...bold.

His fingers weaved the strands together effortlessly, the gentle graze of them against my neck making me clear my throat to break the awkward silence.

He gave it a gentle tug.

"That should hold."

Heat flushed my cheeks as I cleared my throat again.

"Thank you."

He hummed in response, grabbing the helmet from my hands and undoing the clasp before sliding it over my head and securing the buckle beneath my chin.

He mounted the bike, gesturing for me to climb on behind him.

I perched on the back of the bike, swinging my leg over and grabbing the sides as hard as I could.

A chuckle came from beneath his helmet, echoing in my own.

I startled, the deep timber of his laugh surrounding me.

"Mics in the helmets, that way we can hear each other when we're on the road. Also, the way you're sitting only works if you plan on ending up in the middle of the street."

I scooched closer, still trying to maintain a decent distance between our bodies. He shook his head, reaching both arms behind him and hooking them beneath my knees, pulling me in one smooth motion until my body was flush against his. Moving his arms up, he grabbed mine and brought them around him to rest on his stomach.

"Like this. Anything less puts you in danger. Got it?"

I nodded, my bulky helmet nearly smacking into his, and was met with another deep chuckle that felt like it was right in my ear.

I think I'm already in danger.

***

We pulled against the curb of a quaint cottage. White stone made up the outside, while thick, dark-stained wood framed out the windows and the door. Bundles of vines trailed across the small roof hanging over the porch. The yard was filled with blossoming dahlias and asters, the reds and oranges of the flowers matching the leaves on the towering oak trees on either side of the yard. We followed the short path of mosaic pavers to the front door, my nerves winding tight in my gut as we approached. Radley didn't bother knocking, just pushed open the door and walked in, reaching for my hand and pulling me in behind him.

"Mom?"

"In here," a soft voice called from deeper inside the house.

I followed Radley down a small hallway and into a living area where a woman sat on a worn leather couch with a book in her hands.

She lifted her head, a smile warming her face as she saw Radley.

"Hello, honey." Her eyes traveled past him and landed on me.

"And who is this?" She eyed me, a warmth radiating from her. Delicate wrinkles lined the corners of her eyes and mouth, telltale signs of a life filled with joy and laughter. Everything about her was inviting, and the entire house, too, had an inviting energy that seemed to pulse around it.

"This is my friend Cairo."

"Cairo." Vesper smiled as she said the word, and for a moment, I wondered if Radley had been wrong. I could have sworn I'd seen the faintest glimmer of recognition in her eyes, but it vanished just as quickly as it had appeared. "What a beautiful name. I don't believe we've met."

She stuck her hand out in my direction, her head cocked slightly to the side.

My hopes deflated like a balloon.

Of course she didn't remember me. Radley had warned me as much, but it was still disappointing.

I slipped my hand into hers and shook it gingerly.

"It's a pleasure to meet you."

"I think you have. She's related to the Gavins."

"Oh, right, right. Of course. You'll have to excuse me, Cairo. My memory just isn't what it used to be."

She didn't look old enough to have memory issues, not from any medical cause anyway.

"It's no problem, really. You have a lovely home."

"Oh! Well thank you, honey." She glanced around the room, as if trying to see it from a visitor's perspective.

"Will you two be staying? I could fix some breakfast."

"That would be great. Cairo?"

"Yes, please."

"Wonderful. You two just make yourselves at home. " She pinched one of his cheeks playfully as she passed him, eliciting an eye roll and a smile from his beautiful face.

"You okay?" Radley walked over to me with his hands in his pockets, his head tilted toward me as he spoke quietly.

I shrugged. "Yeah. I mean, I didn't remember her either. I guess I'd hoped you were wrong though. How can her best friend not remember her? Or me?"

"I wish I had answers for you."

***

We made small talk with his mom in between bites of French toast and fried eggs, Radley doing most of the talking as I tried to force my attention to stay at the table in front of me.

Everything had the slightest hint of familiarity to it, from the pictures on the walls to the faded dishes we ate off of. I couldn't place anything in a particular memory, despite my best efforts, but I was certain I had been here before. Vesper had the same look on her face a few times while we spoke, the tiniest crease forming around her eyes as her head slanted just a touch and she looked at me like she could find the answers written on my face if she tried hard enough.

After helping her clean up, we said our goodbyes and excused ourselves under the guise of running errands. My chest felt heavy as we closed the front door behind us and walked toward the street.

A light autumn breeze blew dried leaves across the path beneath our feet, the gentle rustling sound they made as they blew past filling the silence between us.

I ran over the contents of the letter in my head, retracing every word in search of something that could point us in the right direction.

"Her letter mentioned something about a deal my mom made. It was vague, but it might be worth looking into. Any ideas?" Radley handed me my helmet, checking the buckle was secure before responding.

"We just have to be careful. I don't know who was after the two of you back then, so I can't assure you they aren't after you now. As far as I can tell, I'm the only one who remembers you, but we can't be too safe."

He thought for a moment, his jaw working as he pondered before finally saying, "I know someone that might be able to help."

CHAPTER 10:

CAIRO

Radley stopped in front of one of the small brick shops on the square. The tin sign hanging above the door was covered in the same ivy that covered most of the architecture around here, and it had three simple words printed on the front: "Cup and Kettle."

"A tea shop?" I questioned.

"Not just any tea. Magic, remember?" He wagged his eyebrows, a smile quirking the corners of his mouth.

I gave him a doubtful look.

"Right."

"Have a little faith, Cairo," he said as he placed his hand on the small of my back and ushered me inside.

Loud bells chimed over the entrance as we walked through. The floor of the shop was old and warped with age, the heady scent of herbs hanging in the air. Bouquets of dried flowers hung upside down from a pole that ran lengthwise along the ceiling.

Vintage tea cups also hung from the ceiling by different colored strands of worn ribbon, the faded embellishments on the cups catching the light and reflecting onto the rows of shelves full of assorted loose herbs and leaves that lined the walls.

The place was...eclectic.

"Radley Cordova," a warm voice called out.

"Hello, Cheris," he replied, a gentle smile on his face as he embraced the woman.

She was a short, older woman, gray hair springing free in different directions from the loose bun on the top of her head. Her skirt swished around her ankles in layers of mismatched fabric.

"Well looky here. Tell me you finally settled down and found yourself a nice girl?"

"Ah, no. This is Cairo."

I waved at the woman.

"It's nice to meet you."

She eyed me, a knowing look on her face as she nodded her head slowly.

"Likewise, honey. So, what can I do for you today?"

"We need some tea."

She hummed. "I see. Anything in particular?"

"Top shelf, please." Cheris and Radley exchanged a look while I stood there awkwardly. I didn't know what they were talking about, or what "top shelf" tea was, but if he thought it would help, then I would go along with it.

"Alright then, follow me." Cheris turned and walked back behind the counter, disappearing through a beaded curtain as we followed after her.

We entered a small, dark room lit entirely by candles placed along the walls and surfaces. A large hutch leaned against the wall, filled with glass jars all containing a dozen or so tea bags. The jars were all labeled with simple one-word names like "Sleep," "Truth," and "Strength."

Cheris moved to the hutch and turned to face us.

"What do you need?"

"See," Radley replied.

Cheris tapped her nails along the shelves of the hutch as she looked over the jars.

"Interesting choice." She grabbed a jar and set it on the table in the middle of the room.

I watched her as she moved around the room, pulling a tea cup and saucer from a cabinet, collecting a tea pot from a burner I had noticed before, and bringing everything back to the table before gesturing for us both to sit.

Radley pulled a chair out for me, then sat down to my left. He gave me a quick smile and squeezed my hand reassuringly.

Removing a single tea bag from the jar, Cheris placed it in the tea cup and then slowly poured the steaming water from the tea pot over the small sachet of herbs.

It could have been the dim light of the room, or the flicker of the flames from the candle nearest us, but I could swear that I saw colors in the steam that rose out of the cup. Tendrils of a deep purple smoke intertwining with black for just a moment, before they evaporated into the air. I narrowed my eyes as I studied the cup, jumping at the sound of metal hitting the porcelain.

I glanced up to see Cheris tapping the side of the cup lightly with a long silver spoon. She clicked it against the side three times, then submerged the spoon and gave it three quick stirs to the left, three to the right, and pulled it out.

"Which of you will be partaking?"

Radley turned his head to look at me. "Trust me?" he asked.

Did I? I chewed at my bottom lip, my foot tapping quietly against the floor. I did. Maybe that was stupid, maybe my intuition was faulty, but I trusted him.

"Yes." The words came out as a whisper.

He smiled at me, his hand reaching under the table to rest on my thigh where he gave it a light squeeze. Heat pulsed from the places of contact between his hand and my leg, and I stifled a gasp as I slapped my hand over his. Our eyes locked, confusion evident in his, but buried beneath a heavy layer of something else. Something…more. I didn't have time to put a name to it, as Cheris cleared her throat from across the table. Both of our heads whipped toward her, a flush creeping onto my cheeks at the knowing look on her face.

"Shall we begin?" she asked, a sly smile playing at the corners of her mouth.

I nodded, accepting the cup as she slid it toward me.

No turning back now.

CHAPTER 11:

CAIRO

"Drink. Slowly, and let it warm you."

I removed my hand from Radley's, noting that he kept his gentle grip on my leg, and lifted the cup to my lips with both hands. I blew out a breath, closing my eyes and letting the liquid tip into my mouth.

A burst of flavors exploded on my tongue, bergamot and cinnamon followed by a sickly sweet fruity flavor and notes of something pungently floral.

"The whole cup," Cheris encouraged, her eyes watching me intently as I swallowed another mouthful.

A tingling started in my fingertips, spreading slowly like warm honey into my arms and coating every vein in my body. I felt my eyelids begin to flutter as I tipped the cup to get the last drop, setting it back down on the saucer and wiping my lips with the back of my hand.

A weightlessness had settled over me, a similar feeling to when I'd had a head cold and took entirely too much cough syrup, resulting in a fuzzy haze that I floated in for hours. This felt kind of like that, but…lighter. The warmth spreading through my body felt like the embodiment of sunlight, bright and clean as it coursed through me. I forced my eyes open, looking first to Radley.

He let out a low whistle.

"Look at those pupils," he chuckled, rubbing gentle circles on my leg reassuringly.

"I feel…" I started, trying to find the words to explain what I was experiencing.

"I know. You'll be okay, Cai. It doesn't last long."

I nodded, but the motion made my head swim. Radley slid his hand across me, pulling my chair closer to his and banding his arm over both of my legs like a seatbelt.

"I've got you," he whispered, just loud enough for me to hear.

"Are you ready to begin?" Cheris asked from across the table.

I forced my eyes to meet hers and nodded.

"I want you to close your eyes, clearing your mind as best you can."

I followed her instructions, letting my eyes close, and taking deep breaths to clear my mind. It was easier than I expected, the haziness of the tea aiding me in losing track of any thoughts I had racing around up there.

"Now, I want you to picture a large glass ball. Give as much detail to it as you please. This is where you will experience the 'see' part of this. Let me know when you have it?"

I focused all of my attention on the ball, imagining a smooth orb of glass, cradled in a brass base. The glass started out colorless and opaque, but the longer I focused on it, the more the color shifted. A lilac tinted smoke swirling through the center of it.

"What color is it, Cairo?" Cheris called.

"It's lilac. It's like smoke, trapped inside of it."

"Good, very good." I could hear the faint sounds of a pen scratching against paper as Cheris spoke.

"Look into it. The smoke is shifting, showing you what it wants you to see. Watch it."

My brows drew together as I watched the smoke transform. It swirled in circles until it coated the entire inside of the glass, and then parted. In the center of the smoke, a distorted vision began to play out.

Two women, both of them older than I am now, speaking in hushed tones, their bodies close together as they spoke. Whatever they were talking about, they didn't want to be overheard.

"We can't come back, Vesper. That was the deal. He has seen the prophecy, he won't stop."

I gasped as the voice echoed in my mind, my hand jumping to Radley's arm and gripping it tightly.

"Breathe, Cai. Just focus, and breathe."

"There has to be something else we can do, Alice. We can't lose the two of you."

"I'm sorry. The bargain has already been made. If we leave, then she stays safe."

The image fizzled out, along with the voices and the image of the globe.

I blinked my eyes open slowly, feeling the tears that had tracked down my face at the sound of my mother's voice.

My mother.

My chest ached, a desperate desire to hear her speak again filling me with dread.

Radley's free hand came up to wipe away the wetness from my cheek.

"Hey, you okay?" His voice was soft, a gentleness I knew was due to the emotions I was wearing all over my face.

"I'm good." I scrubbed my hands over my face, wiping away the tear tracks that streaked down to my chin.

"Thank you, Cheris." Radley nodded to the woman, who sat with her hands steepled under her chin and her eyes slightly narrowed in my direction.

"She's going to be a little drained after today. Take her home and have her drink this." Cheris handed him a small bag containing a single tea bag and chuckled in response to my audible groan at the sight of another mystical drink.

"This one is just herbal tea, honey. It'll help dispel the effects of what you drank a few minutes ago. Get some rest."

I managed a small smile, offering her a thanks before turning toward the door. Cheris put a hand on Radley's arm as he turned to follow me and leaned in closer to him.

"When she's feeling back to normal, take her to the archives. I think it will help with whatever she's looking for."

Radley nodded and looked to me. "Are you okay to ride back?"

"Yeah, I'm good." I followed him outside, climbing on behind him, securing my helmet and plastering myself to his back. I didn't have the energy to worry about what felt appropriate. Half my body still felt like Jell-O and if wrapping myself around him kept me on that bike, then fine.

He kicked the motorcycle into gear and pulled out onto the road, the ride back to his house nearly lulling me to sleep.

Or actually lulling me to sleep.

"Cai?" Radley was patting at my hands around his stomach as his voice echoed through the speakers in the helmet I wore.

"We're here."

I forced myself to sit up from where I'd slumped against his back and dismounted the bike.

After making it inside, I followed Radley into the kitchen. I pushed myself up to sit on the counter while he puttered around the room, collecting a mug and a kettle and preparing the tea for me.

He added a cube of sugar, stirring it intently with a spoon before handing the mug to me.

"It'll help, trust me."

"You've done that before? The crazy tea, I mean."

He rubbed at the back of his neck.

"Ahh, yeah. A few times. It never gets any easier." A chuckle fell from his lips.

A comfortable silence settled over us as I sipped from the mug in my hands. I knew I needed to discuss everything I had seen and heard, but the vivid image of my mother and the sound of her voice in my head felt so…raw. Her voice was so achingly vulnerable and afraid as she spoke, but there was no denying the determination there either. She was leaving, and she was taking me with her.

"Do you want to talk about it?" he asked.

"Yes. But I can't right now, it's too fresh. Her voice." I waved my hand around my head and shrugged, indicating what a mess the inside of my mind was at the moment.

"I get it. Want to check out the archives then? It's not far."

"Sure." I finished the tea in the mug and set it in the sink before shaking the grief from my shoulders and heading out the door after Radley in search of more answers.

CHAPTER 12:

CAIRO

A massive stone building stood in front of me, towering steeples jutting from the top of the black shingled roof. Ivy climbed up the front of the structure in rows, covering large portions and giving the illusion that this place was entirely abandoned. Gothic-style windows were placed on either side of the entrance doors, the black wood of the frames weathered and chipped. It was gorgeous. Part of me wondered if anyone ever kept up with this place, but the other part of me was mesmerized by the beauty of it.

Radley placed his hand at the small of my back and guided me through the doors, revealing an interior just as breathtaking, though less abandoned-looking. Long, heavy wooden tables lay in rows on one side of the room and bookshelves wrapped around the inside on almost every wall. Thick books sat on every shelf, some of them so old that the binding had faded and the titles were barely visible. To the left, a woman sat behind a tall counter. Her gray hair was cut short and styled into roller curls and she was wrapped in a cardigan two sizes too big for her. She smiled warmly as she lifted her head and noticed us.

"Oh, Radley!" She beamed at him. I was beginning to realize that everyone knew him. He was adored, at least by the older women in this town.

"Hello, Nell." He inclined his head toward her.

Her gaze slid to me, then immediately back to Radley.

Okay then.

"Anything I can help you with?"

"Yes, actually. I need a key to the back room."

She pursed her lips, cocking her head to the side slightly as she looked at him.

"Do I dare ask what for?"

"Better if you don't," he said with a wink.

She sighed, shaking her head at him like he was an unruly toddler before retrieving a key from her pocket and placing it in his hand. She dismissed us with a wave, her nose already buried back in the book in her hand.

He led me to the back of the building and through a substantial wooden door against the back wall. It lead to a stuffy little room, an office desk crammed into one corner and a table taking up the majority of the leftover space. The table was piled high with dust-covered books, particles floating in the stagnant air as I moved around the room, searching for anything useful.

"What are we looking for in here, exactly?" I asked, watching as he slowly made his way around the small room.

"This is where they used to keep all of the older books on the town's history. I guess they moved them since the last time I was in here." He sighed, the crease between his brow deepening.

The chain around my neck warmed, so subtle I didn't pay it any attention at first. I kept moving around the room, searching every book title for something that stood out. I let my fingers trail along the wall as I moved, the cool stone a welcome contrast to the growing heat around my neck. I made it halfway around the room when the charm dangling between my breasts let out a zap strong enough to startle a yelp out of me. I jumped back, clutching at the fabric of my shirt and pulling it away from my skin.

"What? What's wrong?" Radley rushed over, a panicked look on his face.

"The necklace, it-it fucking shocked me." I stared at it in bewilderment.

"The necklace?"

"It was my mom's. It did this when I first put it on, and on the way into Hadeon, but it hasn't done anything since. I thought it was static or something, but it's hot, Radley. Feel it." My brain clearly wasn't functioning properly at the moment because I grabbed his hand and shoved it down my shirt and over the charm.

His eyes shot wide and his eyebrows raised as he stared at me.

"Cai, what are you doing?"

"Feel it! Can't you feel how hot it is?"

"It just feels like a necklace to me. It's cold." His hand was stone still as I clutched it to my chest.

Embarrassment at what I had just done seeped in as I slowly removed his hand, smoothing the neckline of my shirt back into place and clearing my throat as I turned around.

My brow furrowed. How could he not feel that? The closer I got to a certain spot in the room, the hotter the jewelry grew against my skin.

I moved slowly, taking cautious steps until I found the area that made the necklace burn the hottest.

"Right here." I ran my hands along the wall, feeling a ripple of energy across it. "There's something right here." Radley stood behind me, searching the wall for something before clicking his tongue and nodding like he'd decided something. He rested his hands on my upper arms, gripping them lightly in support.

"We're going to try something, okay?"

"Okay?"

"It's probably going to sound crazy to you, but I just need you to trust me, Cai."

"Okay."

"Close your eyes."

I nodded and exhaled, doing as he said. "Imagine the wall as a door, focus as hard as you can, and push against it."

"With my hands?"

"No, imagine something inside of you, a stream of water, a line of fire, whatever helps you focus, and push it toward the door."

I squeezed my eyes tight, focusing all my energy on finding the thing inside me I could use to attempt this, while at the same time trying to push the ludicrousness of this whole charade out of my mind.

I shook my head; this was useless. There was nothing there and I felt silly.

Radley lowered his head so that his chin was resting on my shoulder.

"Relax, Cai." His deep voice sent a shiver skirting down my spine, the gentleness he spoke with was such a stark contrast to the rough pitch of his voice.

"It's there. You just have to find it." He rubbed his hands up and down my arms.

"Okay, I've got this."

"You've got this. I'm pushing too, it's not all on you. Just try to feel it," he agreed encouragingly.

I blocked out everything but the feeling of the necklace, hot against my skin. A thin tendril of pure energy appeared in my mind. I pulled against it, marveling at the iridescent blue color. The harder I focused, the larger it grew, doubling in size until it resembled the body of a large snake. Shades of blue ranging from deep and royal to an aquamarine swirled along its mass, the colors shifting effortlessly as I pulled it toward me.

I tried to grab a hold of it mentally, failing miserably.

Finally, I gritted my teeth and shoved at it as hard as I could, willing it toward the wall in front of me.

The necklace pulsed, the rhythm in line with my erratic heartbeat.

"Holy shit," Radley whispered in awe.

The wall had vanished, like it was never there at all. In its place stood a tall doorway, leading into a cavernous stone room. The ceilings stretched high above the main area of the library, explaining the tall steeples outside. I took a cautious step over the threshold, feeling a thin barrier push against me gently before falling away.

I turned my head to look back at Radley who still stood in the same spot, his shocked gaze locked on the room before us.

"It's okay, come on." I gestured for him to follow me as I entered the room fully.

It was breathtaking. A beam of light poured down through a skylight in the middle of the ceiling, casting a warm glow around the room.

Bookshelves had been carved into the stone walls, holding hundreds of ancient tomes. I ran my fingers along the spine of a faded blue book sitting on a shelf to my right, surprised when my fingers came away free of dust.

Sconces on the wall flared to life as we walked to the center of the room where a small wooden table stood, a massive book open on a stand on its surface.

We stood side-by-side, both of us feeling the energy that vibrated from the book in front of us. It felt…heavy. Not necessarily dark, but overwhelming in a way that made me want to run.

I touched my hands to the weathered pages, sucking in a breath as a hum built beneath my fingertips. Radley watched me carefully as I drew my hand back and cleared my throat.

And then I read from the book aloud.

CHAPTER 13:
THE PROPHECY

From the ashes of the forgotten past,
A flame shall rise, fierce and fast.
Bound by a tether of ancient might,
The one of Shadows will bring forth Light.

Through trials steeped in pain and loss,
She will mend the cracks and bridge the cross.
A heart divided must be made whole,
Her sacrifice will save the soul.

When Darkness strikes its final chord,
The key will lie in the bond restored.
For only together can the cycle reset,
And peace return where chaos met.

CHAPTER 14:

CAIRO

Prophecy?
I had heard that word, in the nightmare, and in…the tea shop. That was what my mother had said.

"He's seen the prophecy."

I could feel myself starting to hyperventilate. The air seemed to grow thicker by the second as I forced it in and out of my lungs. I gripped the sides of the table, leaning over it to ease the ache building under my ribs.

"Cairo, hey, look at me." Radley held my face between his hands, tilting my head to look me in the eyes as he spoke.

"Whatever this is, we will figure it out." Panic clutched me painfully.

"Is…is that about…me?" I stumbled over the words as they left my mouth, my breathing ragged.

"It definitely sounded familiar, but we don't know anything for sure. Look at me, Cairo." I forced my eyes to meet his, my vision tunneling as the weight of the prophecy sunk in. "I will rip that damn thing to shreds myself if that is the only solution, do you understand? We will find answers, loopholes, a fucking wizard if that's what it takes, but you are not alone in this." There was a defiant determination in his words. I didn't believe he had the power to stop the prophecy, but I sure as hell believed he'd do everything in his power to try.

I nodded weakly, my breaths still coming in short pants.

"Words, Cai. Tell me you understand you aren't in this alone."

"I…understand," I gasped. My head was spinning. Was this why my mom had run? Because I was destined to make some sort of sacrifice? Bits and pieces of the words I had read floated around my head. A sacrifice. Darkness. An ancient tether. A dull ache sizzled in my veins, the feeling coursing through my entire body as I shook with both hands planted on the table.

Radley ran worried eyes over my face and he shook his head back and forth like he was at a loss.

The ache turned into a throb, picking up momentum by the second and after a few labored breaths, I felt like my body was on fire from the inside out.

"Radley," I choked out, rubbing furiously at the heat beneath my skin. "It's burning! I'm burning!" I could hear the panic in my voice, and the look on his face told me he could too. Lava surged through my veins, scorching its way through my body and boiling every nerve it touched.

"What is? The necklace?" He lifted the chain with his fingers, pulling it away from my body as he spoke.

"No, me! I'm burning!"

"Oh, fuck." Recognition dawned in his eyes. He knew what was happening.

"It's your Variance." He held my chin, turning my head side to side as he observed my eyes before swearing under his breath and pulling out his phone. He swiped at the screen a few times before raising it to his ear.

"Are you home?" He waited for a reply on the other end of the line, his brows knitted together in worry and concentration.

"Meet me at my house. Her Variance just emerged."

He used his free hand to push the hair back from my face, resting his hand on the back of my neck and keeping his eyes locked with mine. I focused on the golden flecks speckled throughout the vivid green of his irises, the low light of the sconces reflecting off of them and stealing my attention away for just a heartbeat.

"Okay, we'll be there soon."

He ended the call, quickly stuffing his phone back in his pocket.

"It's not fair to have this explained to you while you're in the middle of it, but I'm just going to hit the main points for right now, okay?" He braced his hands on my shoulders, demanding my full attention before he continued.

I jerked my head up and down.

"Your Variance, your particular strain of magic, is emerging and it's a bitch, I won't lie to you. Jax and I both went through it, but it's easier if you aren't alone. We're going to go to my house so we can help you through it."

"Does everyone here—" I started, but he cut me off with a quick shake of his head.

"No. That's why we're going to Jax. He'll keep it between us for now."

"Okay." The word came through gritted teeth as I fought back the scream that was building in my throat. I felt like I was being gutted, ice and fire battling through my body.

He shrugged off his jacket, wrapping it around my shoulders and reaching for my hands that still had a white-knuckled grip on the table. I managed to pry them loose, grabbing onto his wrist with my left hand.

And immediately taking the first normal breath I'd had in the last ten minutes.

We both reeled back at the static that rippled from the point of contact between my palm and his wrist.

Right where his star was.

Oh.

Oh, fuck.

"Radley..." I whispered, the idea of voicing what was going through my mind currently too much to handle. There was going to be an explanation for that. Just one single thing in this town that made sense.

"Yup. That's...that." His nostrils flared and his jaw tightened as he scrubbed his free hand over his mouth.

CHAPTER 15:

RADLEY

Fuck.

Fuck. Fuck. Fuck.

"We need to go, okay?"

She nodded her head weakly as I wrapped my arm around her waist and guided her back toward the entrance to the room. As we stepped over the threshold, I turned my head to watch as the brick wall that had kept it concealed quickly reappeared, closing it off once again. Unease worked its way through my mind, but that was a problem for another time.

I ushered Cairo back out of the archives, muttering useless apologies under my breath as I strapped the helmet on her head and settled her on the back of my bike before swinging my leg over and mounting it.

She wrapped her arms tightly around my stomach, her fingers ice-cold through the thin fabric of my shirt. I tugged the hem of it up, nudging her clasped hands higher on my abdomen and pulling the fabric over them. Her sigh of relief echoed through the speakers in my helmet, the sound so content it eased some of the tension in my shoulders.

I made the drive back to my house in record time, screeching to a stop in front of the garage as Jax came running down the front steps, a blanket already in his hands.

I climbed off my bike, reaching out for Cairo and pulling her into my arms, her hand instantly reaching for my wrist, almost as if on instinct.

"Dude, what the hell is going on?"

"Just help me get her inside. She's freezing. We need to get her in the tub."

Jax tucked the blanket around her shoulders, giving her a reassuring smile when her eyes slid to him.

"Hey, trouble." He grinned at her, evoking a small smile from her lips in return.

"You hanging in there okay?" Her chin quivered as she jerked a nod, tugging the blanket tighter around her shoulders.

The three of us hustled through the house and up the stairs to my bedroom and into the bathroom suite. He started the bath, running hot water before stepping back with a hand on his neck.

"What do I do?" he asked

"Just hang out for a second in case I need you."

I pulled at the blanket wrapped around her, letting it hit the floor before pulling back to strip some of the layers off of both of us.

She whimpered quietly as I moved my hand away and she lost contact with my mark, a frown forming on my face as I hurried to get the jacket and sweater off of her before offering her my wrist again. Jax stood to the side, observing the interaction with wide eyes.

"Did that just—"

"Not now," I gritted out. The last thing we needed was this getting out. As far as I knew, an actual bond mark wasn't just rare, it was completely unheard of. It was for fairytales.

Cairo stood in her jeans and a tank top, her teeth chattering together as I pulled my shirt over my back, kicking off my shoes and stepping into the hot water. I sucked a breath in through my teeth at the heat, reaching my hand out to her as she climbed in. I settled into the tub, my legs bent wide and pulled her in between them, her back flush against my chest and my arms around her where she clutched my wrist to her chest with a desperate grip.

I looked to Jax who stood still as a statue, taking in the situation with a mixture of fear and apprehension.

"I've got her. Go to the study and see what books my dad might have had on…bonds."

"Bonds." He repeated the word like it was foreign.

"Yes." The look on my face must have conveyed my impatience because he nodded his head roughly and stumbled out of the room, closing the door softly behind him.

"How are you feeling, Cai?"

"Li-like my body i-is on fire and fr-frozen at the same time."

I grabbed a washcloth from the shelf next to the tub, soaking it in the hot water and squeezing it over her shoulders.

"Is the water helping?"

"You are."

My heart stuttered in my chest, thumping painfully out of rhythm at her words. I knew something was off. I knew when she crossed that barrier, the mark on my wrist burning like I'd held it to a flame. I'd tried to push it out of my mind, there was no way that she'd actually managed that kind of magic—ancient, forbidden magic—at eight years old.

Yet, here we were.

She rolled to her side on my chest, tucking her head in the hollow of my neck and taking the first deep breath I'd heard since we entered the archives.

"What's happening to me, Radley." It was more a statement than a question, which was good because I didn't have the slightest fucking clue how to answer that.

"We'll figure it out. I promise."

I dipped the washcloth in the water again, squeezing it out over her back and rubbing it over her arm.

She sighed into my neck, the feel of her warm breath making me grit my teeth against the bodily reaction it was causing in me.

And now really wasn't the time, but God, she was beautiful.

She always had been, even when we were kids I was mesmerized by her. Those grey eyes and wild curls had sucked me in from the day I met her.

But now? She was gorgeous. The last time I saw her she was missing more than one tooth, all lanky limbs and skinned knees. The woman in my arms now, she was a goddess. The curves of her body molded to me in a way that set my heart rate at a dangerous pace. I gave into temptation, carefully tugging the hair tie from the end of her braid and running my fingers through her long hair. She hummed in response.

"What is a Variance?"

I blew out a breath. How do you explain something like this to someone who didn't even know magic existed until a few days ago?

"It's like a strain of magic. The Gods, they were the power sources for every kind of magic hundreds of years ago. When they went away, the magic began to dwindle. It diluted throughout bloodlines, until eventually certain kinds of magic vanished altogether. Now, most people have very menial abilities. They might be able to move a pencil across the table, or light a candle with a flick of their wrist, but that is the extent of their power. There are very few people who still develop potent Variances, and even then they are nothing like they used to be."

"You and Jax both have them?"

"Yes. It's something we learn about around the time we're in high school here so that we are prepared for the possibility. We are warned about the pain that can accompany an emerging Variance, so it isn't quite as jarring for us as it was for you. I'm sorry for that."

"Not your fault," she mumbled.

"We're going to get you through it."

"I know." Her voice was little more than a whisper, her body melting fully against mine.

I wrapped my arms around her tighter, content to answer her questions or hold her like this, whichever she needed more right now.

Her body returned to a normal temperature around the same time her heart rate slowed back down. Her deep, even breaths told me she was asleep, but safe.

I let my head fall back against the edge of the tub and closed my eyes.

A knock sounded at the bathroom door, and I opened one eye as Jax walked back in. He looked from Cairo's sleeping form to my face, his lips pulled into a tight line.

"I found something."

CHAPTER 16:

RADLEY

I managed to keep Cairo awake long enough to change into a pair of dry sweatpants and a loose shirt I pulled from my closet, her eyes drooping as I handed them to her and promised to wait on the other side of the door. She came out looking like she hadn't slept in months, walking to me and smushing her face against my chest with her hands tucked under her chin, and uttered one simple word.

"Bed."

I carried her to the spare bedroom she had claimed, tucking her under the heavy blankets. I hadn't even made it to the bedroom door before she was fast asleep.

I jogged down the stairs, meeting Jax in the small sitting room where he sat in an oversized armchair, his hands steepled under his chin and his leg bouncing frantically.

"How is she?" He stood as I walked in.

"Asleep. Her Variance was…delayed. On top of that, she had no idea what was happening so the adrenaline added to it. She'll be fine in a few hours."

He bobbed his head, thumping his knuckles against the stack of books on the coffee table beside him.

"Good. Now explain to me why the only references I can find in your father's study to a mark that eases an Emergence are in fables?"

I worked my jaw back and forth as he glared at me. Trusting Jax wasn't an issue; he was like a brother to me. Saying what was actually happening out loud, giving life to it, though, that was another thing altogether.

I plopped down in the seat across from him, crossing my arms over my chest and meeting his stare head on.

"Because bonds aren't supposed to exist outside of those books."

"They aren't *supposed* to?"

I shook my head slowly.

"Gods, Radley. What have you gotten yourself into?" Tension radiated from his body as he paced in front of the large fireplace. "Every mention of a bond is in a kids' story, or scribbled notes that don't make any sense. They don't exist, Radley, so explain this to me."

"It's not like I asked for it, Jax." A defensive edge creeped into my voice. "It happened when we were kids. She didn't even know what she was doing."

He threw his arms up. "How? How does that happen?"

"I don't know." My words came out louder than intended, and my jaw clenched as I forced myself to take a deep breath. "There are a lot of questions that need answering, but none of them will change what this is."

Jax moved back to the chair, sitting with his head resting in his hands. "Is this why they left? Did someone find out?"

"That would be my guess. My mom never mentioned it, but she never mentioned them at all after they left."

"Maybe her mom knew? You said you were kids when it happened, so maybe she saw it and freaked out and they bolted."

"That explains why they left, but not why no one in this town remembers a woman who lived here her entire life."

I'd found pictures of my mom and Alice, Cairo's mom, in a box of old photographs years ago. When I showed them to her, there wasn't even a glimmer of recognition in her eyes. Just a pinched confusion that stuck to her face for hours afterward.

Later, I came in to find the entire box of photos in the trash.

On the top was a picture of me and Cairo—we couldn't have been more than five—at the small playground beside the elementary school. Cairo sat on a swing, a toothy grin on display as she pointed her toes toward the sky. I stood behind her, my arms still outstretched from the push I'd given her before the picture was snapped.

That one sat in the back of my wallet, the same place it had been since the day I found it.

"There's got to be more to it, we just have to figure out where else to look." Jax turned pensive, his usually lighthearted attitude nowhere to be found beneath the hard layers of fear and curiosity he currently wore.

"I need to find out who was after them before they left. If they're still around, then we're going to have to be careful with how we go about this."

"She's going to need help with her Variance, either way."

"Yeah, I was hoping maybe you'd want to stick around for that. I can't tell what hers is yet, and I figure the two of us together have a better shot at countering it if it's as strong as I'm thinking it will be."

"Strong enough to make her and her mom run?"

"Strong enough to make them disappear."

CHAPTER 17:

CAIRO

The afternoon sun streamed through the towering oak trees, casting long, golden beams across the forest floor. I stood at the center of the dirt circle Radley had drawn with a stick, sweat clinging to my forehead and my breathing labored from the last round of practice. Radley moved in front of me, his own chest rising and falling in a steady rhythm. His dark hair was tousled, and a hint of a grin played at the corner of his lips as he watched me attempt to catch my breath. He raised an eyebrow, eyes dancing with challenge.

"You're getting there," he assured me, voice low and smooth. "I can feel it."

A flicker of warmth that had nothing to do with magic thrummed through me, the space between us charged with something far beyond spells and control. I met his gaze, refusing to look away despite the heat that crept up my neck.

"I don't think we're feeling the same thing then," I said, the edge in my voice a result of the nerves I kept trying to choke down. Each time I pushed, the magic responded, but it was sporadic and wild. I didn't have any semblance of control over it, and that terrified me. I had spent the first hour feeling ridiculous. Magic practice? I kept waiting for the camera crews to jump out and tell me this had all been an elaborate prank.

Realistically, how long does it take for someone to accept that something like this exists?

However long that is, I needed twice that amount of time.

I had finally loosened up, unable to refute the buzzing in my veins as Radley walked me through how to call the magic to the surface. It's hard to deny something when you can literally feel it in you, in your very core.

"Go again." Radley's tone left no room for argument as he backed up to the edge of the circle and gestured for me to get on with it. My goal was to produce a steady stream of fire and direct it at the pile of sticks in the center of the circle. So far, I hadn't managed to get within more than a foot of it.

I closed my eyes, forcing deep breaths in and out of my lungs. The prophecy ran through my mind on an unwelcome loop, each word causing the dread in my stomach to double until I felt like I'd swallowed a brick of lead. Sweat beaded on my neck, trickling down over my hammering pulse as I tried to regain my focus.

The fire lashed out before I could stop it, wild and hot, tearing through the air between us like a bullet. My heart sank to my feet as Radley threw up his hands, his own magic forming a shimmering black barrier. The flames smacked into it, sizzling and roaring, before fizzling out into smoke.

My hands gripped at the roots of my hair as I waited for the barrier to dissipate and see if he'd been injured. He pulled his magic back, walking toward me with his hands out to show me he was okay, but tears still stung my eyes.

"Stop," he said, his voice calm but firm. He stood in front of me, holding his hands out like he wanted to take mine. "Cairo, it's fine."

"It's not fine!" I hissed, looking anywhere but at him. My breath came fast and jagged, like shards of glass scraping my throat. "I could've burned you. I could've—"

"But you didn't," he interrupted. "I am fine. Let me help you."

I finally looked at him then, at the faint scorch marks on his forearms, the sweat beading at his temple. He wasn't fine. And it was my fault. Shame beat at the back of my mind, but I nodded anyway.

Radley reached out, his fingers brushing my wrists, and a warmth spread through me, gentle and steady unlike the fire I had yet to control. The tendrils of his magic wrapped around mine, soothing the raw edges of whatever had broken loose inside. For a moment, I felt like I could breathe again.

"I can't control it."

"You can," he urged, his tone even, like it was a fact carved in stone. "We just don't know how yet."

I wanted to believe him, I ached to believe him.

But in the back of my mind, a voice whispered, *What if I'm meant to destroy everything I touch?*

Frustration boiled in my veins, a burning desire to control something I didn't even know existed until a few days ago.

Power raced from my fingertips, blasting into the ground at my feet and sending dirt and rocks flying upward. A clump of torched grass smacked into my outstretched palm, searing the skin and my dignity.

Well, shit.

CHAPTER 18:

RADLEY

The bathroom was too small for Cairo's magic. The walls still held the vague smell of smoke, though I'd thrown open the window to clear the air. Cairo sat on the counter, her legs dangling over the edge, cradling her burned hand in her lap. She wouldn't look at me.

"How is it feeling?" I asked, grabbing a clean wash cloth from under the sink.

"I'm fine," she muttered, her voice brittle. "It was a stupid misfire."

I turned, and the sight of her made my chest tighten. Her hair was disheveled, stray wisps clinging to her damp forehead, and her cheeks were streaked with soot. Her left hand, the one she was clutching, was angry red, blistering at the edges. A misfire, she'd called it. A bad one.

"Let me see," I said, setting the cloth down next to her. When she didn't move, I crouched in front of her, close enough that I could see the slight tremble in her shoulders. "Cairo. Let me see."

She exhaled sharply and held out her hand. The burn was worse than I thought—deep, spreading up her palm and wrist. I bit back a curse.

"I've had worse." Her voice was too quiet, too small for her.

I ignored her, setting my hands lightly over the burn. My magic stirred, warm and golden, weaving into the damaged skin. She flinched, but I didn't stop, letting the light seep deeper, pulling the edges of the wound back together.

"How are you doing that?"

"Part of my Variance. All I'm doing is pushing my magic into you. It heals minor injuries," I told her, my voice low as I concentrated. "We need to work on your control. Frustration is a given while you're learning to use your abilities, and we can't have you charring yourself every time you get pissed."

Her eyes snapped to mine, and for a moment, she looked like she wanted to argue. Then she just shook her head. "I know. I'm just…I'm trying."

"I know you are." I glanced at her other hand, still smudged with soot, and reached for a clean towel. "And you're doing so good, Cai. You don't see it, but you have faced everything in this town head on. That's more than most people would do. You'll get better at this, it just takes time."

"I don't want to hurt anyone," she whispered.

The words hit harder than they should have. I paused, the towel halfway to her arm. "You didn't hurt me."

"Not this time, but I have to get a grip on this, Radley. My only option is to keep going, to get stronger and manage all of this," she said, waving her good hand around, her voice breaking. "But what if next time I——?"

I didn't let her finish. "Stop." I straightened, holding her burned hand in mine, now smooth and whole again. "You're not going to hurt me. And you're not going to hurt anyone else, not if I can help it. When are you going to realize that you aren't alone, Cairo?"

Her lips parted, like she wanted to say something, but all that came out was a shaky breath. I rested my hand on her uninjured one and felt the tremor there.

"You trust me, right?" I asked softly.

She nodded, just barely.

"Good." I gave her hand a light squeeze. "Then let me carry some of this. You don't have to hold it all on your own."

For the first time since I'd brought her in, she let her shoulders drop. Her legs stopped swinging, and she leaned forward just enough that her forehead brushed my chest. I didn't say a word, I just wrapped my arms around her shoulders and let her rest there while the room settled into silence.

The fire in her was dangerous, unpredictable, but it wasn't her enemy. And neither was I.

Suddenly, Cairo's magic burned through the air between us, wild and untamed, and for a second, I thought I wouldn't be fast enough. I threw up a shield, feeling the searing heat press against it before it died out. The look on her face—wide-eyed and terrified—hurt worse than the sting of the flames.

She had curled in on herself like she wanted to disappear. "I didn't mean to," she whimpered, her voice shaking.

"I know," I replied, forcing my tone to stay calm, even though my pulse was still racing.

She wouldn't look at me. I hated that. Cairo just had this aura about her, so fearless, so sure of herself—until her magic started tearing her apart. Doubt lingered at her edges, just waiting for her to mess up in a big enough way that it would consume her. I wouldn't let that happen.

I rested my chin on the top of her head, savoring the rise and fall of her shoulder as the adrenaline left her body.

"You are powerful," I said. "There is a reason for that."

She didn't say anything, just nodded. I could tell she was still afraid—of herself, of what she might do. But I wasn't afraid of her. Not for a second.

If we had to chase down the beings who made that prophecy to get answers, then that's what we would do. For her, I'd face anything.

Cairo stayed slumped against me for a minute, her breathing evening out. I didn't move, letting her take what she needed. When she finally leaned back, her eyes looked tired, but the tightness in her shoulders seemed to have eased somewhat.

"Better?" I asked.

She nodded, rubbing her newly healed hand. "Thanks."

I closed the first-aid kit and straightened up. The air in the bathroom felt leaden, like the weight of her magic lingered in the walls, and I knew if I didn't do something, she'd spiral back into her head. Again.

"Alright," I said, leaning against the counter and crossing my arms. "Get your shoes."

She blinked at me, looking confused. "What?"

"You heard me. Shoes, jacket. Let's go."

Her eyebrows furrowed. "Go where?"

"Into town," I answered, as if it were obvious. "You need ice cream."

"Ice cream?" she repeated, like I'd just suggested a trip to the moon. "Radley, I literally just scorched myself. Why on earth would I want ice cream?"

"Because it's impossible to be upset while eating ice cream," I said, grabbing a clean towel to dry my hands. "It's science."

She scoffed, though it sounded more like an amused huff. "That's not science."

"Then it's magic," I retorted, shooting her a grin. "And since we both have magic, it should work twice as well."

She shook her head, muttering something about me being ridiculous, but I caught the faintest hint of a smile tugging at her lips.

"I don't know…" she started, her voice hesitant. "What if I…what if it happens again?"

"It won't," I said firmly. "And if it does, I'll be there. Plus, if you accidentally set fire to something, it'll just be a cone. Ice cream melts anyway."

"Radley." She gave me a flat look, but I caught the way her shoulders shook with a suppressed laugh.

"C'mon," I urged, nudging her foot with mine. "You've had a rough day. You deserve a break. Let's go before the place closes."

She hesitated, like she wanted to argue, but finally sighed and hopped off the counter.

"Fine. But if this is some sneaky attempt to make me feel better—"

"Then it's already working," I finished for her, grabbing her jacket off the hook by the door.

Her smile this time was small but real. "You're insufferable."

"True," I said, holding the door open for her. "But you like me anyway."

She rolled her eyes but didn't deny it, and for the first time that day, I felt like we'd found a sliver of normal.

CHAPTER 19:

CAIRO

The autumn air nipped at my face as we walked, crisp and sharp, each breath helping to clear my head. I shoved my hands deep into my jacket pockets, letting my eyes drift over the town. It felt like I was seeing it for the first time, even though I'd apparently lived here for a decent portion of my life.

Golden light spilled from shop windows, catching on the cobblestones. Clusters of pumpkins sat on stoops, their bright orange shells softened by the haze of dusk. It was a beautiful town, a picture-perfect postcard setting that seemed to glow as we made our way down the sidewalk.

Radley walked beside me, his hands in his own pockets, steps easy and unhurried. He didn't say much at first, and I was grateful for the silence. My hand still tingled where he'd healed it, the skin cool and whole again, but I couldn't stop thinking about the moment it had burned.

The fire had felt alive, wild, like it wasn't just part of me but something bigger. Something I couldn't control. It was terrifying. Whatever my role was here, it had been decided for me a long time ago. I couldn't walk away, so I had to figure out a way to control new parts of me that I didn't know existed without hurting the people I cared about.

"You good?" Radley's voice cut into my thoughts.

I shrugged, kicking at a stray leaf. "Yeah. I just wish I could remember this place."

"Well, now you get to experience it all over again."

I didn't reply, but I could feel his gaze on my face even when I wasn't looking at him.

As we turned onto Main Street, I noticed the people first. They were everywhere—sitting at small tables outside the coffee shop, chatting on the benches on the square, walking hand-in-hand. Some of them smiled and nodded at Radley as we passed.

"Evening, Radley," one woman said, her voice friendly. Her eyes flicked to me for half a second before darting away.

"Evening," he said back, his tone casual.

It was something that kept happening. Small waves, polite nods, glances that lingered a little too long. They didn't recognize me, but they all knew Radley. And because I was with him, they looked.

"How long until the new girl on the block thing wears off?" I muttered, keeping my eyes on the ground.

"Honestly, we've never had a new girl," he replied. "So it's hard to say."

I shrugged again, my steps quickening. "It's weird, like I'm invisible and under a spotlight at the same time."

"They're not staring at you." His voice was soft. "They're just curious. They know you aren't quite..."

He stopped himself, but I already knew what he meant.

"Like them," I finished for him. The bitterness in my voice surprised me.

"That's not it," he said, his tone even. "They don't recognize you, which is odd around here. Part of them wonders who you are, part of them is wondering how the hell you got here, and the rest of it is cloaked in some kind of mild amnesia that makes them forget they were ever curious in the first place after they walk past us."

I pressed my lips together, trying to keep the knot in my chest from tightening. I hated being looked at, especially now.

Radley must have noticed, because he bumped my shoulder lightly. "You want me to cause a scene? I could hit someone. Take your pick and I'll knock them out, put all the attention on me."

I couldn't help it—a short laugh escaped me. "Alright. The old lady over there." I pointed to an elderly woman crossing the street ahead of us.

"Oh, you're sick," he said, grinning again.

By the time we reached the ice cream shop, the pressure in my chest had loosened a little. The bell jingled as we stepped inside, and the warm air enveloped me. It smelled like caramel and chocolate, with a hint of the waffle cones stacked behind the counter.

Radley gestured at the rows of colorful tubs. "What'll it be?"

I stared at the options, overwhelmed. "I don't know...what's good?"

"Everything." He shrugged. "Gotta be some kind of food Variance I don't know about because this," he pointed to the rows of flavors in front of us, "is the best ice cream I've ever had."

I chuckled at the seriousness in his tone. Radley had such an intimidating appearance, the dark hair, the tattoos, even the way he carried himself would have most people thinking twice before they engaged with him. Yet here he was, filled with excitement over an ice cream cone.

I ordered a single scoop of cookie dough ice cream, my go-to flavor since I was a kid. I caught more glances from people sitting by the windows, but this time, they felt shorter, less important. The tension eased from my shoulders, and for a moment, it wasn't about magic or fire or control.

It was just Radley and me, standing in a little shop, figuring out how to breathe again.

CHAPTER 20:

CAIRO

The sun had nearly set by the time we left the ice cream shop. The street lights flickered on, casting warm pools of light onto the cobblestones beneath our feet. I held my empty cone in one hand, my jacket zipped up tight against the chill.

The quiet between us wasn't uncomfortable, it never was, but something about the night felt delicate, like it could break with the wrong move.

And then she appeared.

"Radley?"

Her voice was high and lilting, the kind that made your skin crawl before you even turned around.

A woman stood just ahead of us, stepping out of the doorway to a small shop. Her coat flared as she moved, her sleek blonde ponytail catching the glow of the streetlights.

Jesus, it's Sleepy Hollow Barbie.

"Anna," Radley said, his voice colder than I'd ever heard it.

She smiled, taking slow, deliberate steps toward us. "Wow. It's been a while." She glanced at me briefly, dismissively, before turning her full attention back to him. "I thought maybe you'd left town or something."

The choice of words struck me as odd, considering they couldn't leave.

"Didn't leave," Radley replied. "Just moved on."

Ouch.

Her smile tightened, and for a second, something bitter flashed in her eyes. Then she looked at me again, longer this time, her gaze sliding over me like she was trying to decide what I was worth.

"And this must be why," she said, her tone dripping with mock sweetness. "Interesting choice."

Oop. That was definitely a dig. Rude.

My voice came out sure and calm as I blinked at her.

"I'm Cairo."

Her smile faltered, and for the first time, she actually looked at me. "Okay?"

I tilted my head just enough to match her energy. "Do you have a problem with me, or are you upset with him? Just trying to figure out the situation here before we get into it."

For a second, her expression wavered, but she recovered quickly, turning back to Radley like I wasn't even worth her time.

"You always did like strays." Her voice was colder now.

I snorted into the cone in my hand as I took a bite out of the side, my eyes ping-ponging between the two of them.

"Enough," he said, his voice cutting through the air like a blade.

Anna blinked, clearly startled by the venom in his tone. "Radley, I—"

"No," he interrupted. His voice was sharp, but his face remained neutral as he spoke. "I'm not interested in whatever you have to say. You are wasting your time and embarrassing yourself."

Her mouth opened, then closed again, like she wasn't sure if she wanted to keep fighting or retreat. I took a small step back, letting out a quiet whistle.

"Whatever this is, it's pathetic," he said, his tone calm but ice-cold. "Move on, Anna. We both have."

She flinched at that, her mask of confidence slipping for a fraction of a second. But she recovered quickly, straightening her coat as she glanced between us. "Fine. I was just being polite, but clearly, that's wasted here."

Her eyes flicked to me one last time, narrowed and disdainful before she spun on her heel and walked away, her high heels clicking against the cobblestones like she couldn't leave fast enough.

"Bye, Hannah!" I waved, though she just kept walking.

Rude.

The tension didn't leave immediately, hanging in the air like smoke. Radley turned to me, his hard expression softening as soon as he met my eyes.

"You okay?" he asked.

"I'm fine," I responded. The situation had been amusing, but I was definitely curious about their history. "Curious, but fine."

ANDI BLACK

Radley tilted his head, his lips twitching like he wanted to smile but couldn't quite manage it. "She sure as hell didn't like you."

"Pity." I pursed my lips in a fake pout.

He raised an eyebrow, his gaze steady. "Already pissing off the locals. What will I do with you?"

Radley shook his head in mock defeat, his expression softening further. "Come on," he said, gesturing to the road ahead. "Let's take a walk."

And as we walked, the sharpness of Anna's words faded into the night. Radley didn't look back, and neither did I. That would be a conversation for another night, I supposed.

We walked in silence for a while, the rhythmic crunch of leaves underfoot filling the space between us. The cobblestones gave way to dirt paths as we left the edge of the square, heading toward the quieter outskirts of town. I could still feel the pressure in my chest, leftover from Anna's sharp words and Radley's cold, unwavering response.

But it wasn't Anna that lingered in my mind now. It was him.

"Can I ask you something?" I asked suddenly, the words slipping out before I could stop them.

Radley glanced over, his brow furrowing. "Sure."

"Everyone over fifty in this town seems to adore you," I said, keeping my tone light, even as I watched his reaction carefully. "But people our age, they give you a wide berth or a death stare. What is that about?"

"My last name, mostly," he answered without hesitation.

"Would you care to elaborate on that?" I pressed.

He stopped walking, turning to face me fully. "You don't remember my father, but he was important around here. Until he wasn't. Overnight, he was outcast and as his son, so was I."

I bit the inside of my cheek, mulling over his words. "But the librarian and Cheris, they love you."

Radley nodded, his face unreadable. "The constable, kind of like our sheriff, has this little rag-tag group of lackeys that give some of the older folks a hard time. I keep an eye on it, run his minions off when they give any of the shop owners trouble."

"Ahh, I see," I said.

He studied me for a long moment, his eyes narrowing slightly. "Ask

86

your questions, Cairo. I can see them all over your face."

"What happened in the years I was gone, Radley?" I kept my voice low, afraid to demand too much of him too soon. But something had hardened him, and it made my stomach hurt to imagine what it could have been.

He sighed, his head tilting back to look at the stars as he thought.

"A lot." His jaw worked back and forth as he considered his words. "I lost you, I lost your mom who was like an aunt to me, I lost my dad a few years later." I knew what it felt like to lose people, I knew the way grief sunk into your bones and sapped the joy from your body. "The reason the constable hates me is because of my father."

"What do you mean?"

"My father taught history classes at the high school for years, and they loved him, Cai. One day, the constable shows up and asks for help on a project he's been working on. They spent weeks holed up in my dad's office, papers scattered across the floor while they drank and scribbled in notebooks and argued." He shook his head, shifting his weight to ease the discomfort of the conversation.

"I didn't know then what it was they had found, only that it was big. Suddenly, Dad was an outcast and the constable wasn't coming around anymore. I didn't find out until years later what had actually happened."

"What happened?"

"The 'project' was the prophecy. The constable had somehow found bits and pieces to that puzzle and enlisted my dad to help put them together. Whatever their disagreement was, the constable told everyone that would listen about how my father stole his research. Dad was fired over it. He kept some of his work from their sessions, which is where Anna comes in. We dated for a few weeks, until I found her in my dad's office after she had excused herself to go to the bathroom. Turns out, the entire relationship was fake. The constable had sent her to get close to me so she could retrieve the papers he wanted."

"I'm sorry, Radley."

"Don't be. It all happened years ago. The reputation has lingered though. My last name carries a weight in this town, and that isn't always a good thing. As I got older, certain people made sure I knew that."

I didn't reply; I wasn't sure what to say to that. I knew what loss felt like, that it had the power to change you. Where I withdrew, Radley hardened, and I couldn't fault him for that.

"I guess I just learned how to push before I could be pushed. The reputation I have, I earned. And it doesn't leave much room for people to treat me like shit just because of whose son I am."

"I get it. I don't judge you for it, either," I said softly.

Radley smiled at me, his expression neutral aside from the small flicker of something in his eyes—relief, maybe, or gratitude. The silence stretched between us, intense but not uncomfortable.

We passed under an archway of trees, their bare branches reaching toward one another like skeletal fingers. The air smelled like damp earth and the faint traces of smoke from a fire somewhere nearby, a reminder that summer had fully given way to autumn.

We reached a small park nestled at the edge of the square, the kind of place with wrought-iron benches and ancient oak trees. Radley gestured toward one of the benches, and I sank down gratefully, my legs tired from the walk. He sat beside me, leaning forward with his elbows on his knees.

For a while, neither of us spoke. The quiet felt different here, less tense and more thoughtful, like we were both turning over the same puzzle in our minds. I could still feel the tingle of magic in my fingertips as I rubbed them together.

What would happen if I couldn't control them?

What would happen if we couldn't figure out the prophecy?

I wanted answers to so many questions.

"Do you think they're watching us?" I asked finally, breaking the silence.

Radley turned his head, frowning. "Who?"

"The ones who wrote the prophecy," I said. "The ancient beings. Or whatever they are. Do you think they're out there somewhere, waiting for us to figure it out?"

Radley exhaled slowly, sitting back against the bench. "I don't know. But I wouldn't be surprised."

I stared up at the branches above us, their shadows shifting in the breeze. "What if we're wrong about all of it?"

"We're not."

The certainty in his voice startled me, and I turned to look at him. He wasn't watching the trees or the path ahead—he was watching me, his eyes unyielding.

"We're not wrong, Cairo," he said again. "You're not wrong. This is happening for a reason, whether we understand it or not."

His words settled over me like a blanket, heavy but comforting. I didn't know if he believed them entirely, but he sounded like he did, and that was enough.

CHAPTER 21:

RADLEY

"NO!" Jax slammed his hands down on either side of his plate, rattling the table we were sitting at.

"Why the fuck would you ruin perfectly good pancakes by putting fruit in them? That's got to be like-like a war crime or something."

Cairo descended into a fit of laughter, her shoulders shaking as she struggled to pull herself together. Jax wore a look of indignation, absolutely appalled that she'd added blueberries to the pancake batter this morning.

"This is not a joke, this is serious." He crossed his arms over his chest, a pout starting to form on his face. I smacked him in the shoulder with the back of my hand.

"Eat. She cooked for us, so eat and tell her thank you." A smile threatened to break through my stern exterior at his antics, but my tone was clear enough that he picked up his fork with a grumble and cut into the stack of pancakes on his plate.

"Thank you, Cairo," he mumbled around a mouthful of food.

"You're welcome, you fruit-immune tit." She laughed as she lifted a glass of orange juice to her lips, catching my eyes over the rim where I shot her a wink.

I reveled in the way my flirting made her cheeks flush.

Cairo had such a strong personality. She didn't let anyone push her around, she didn't take shit from anyone, and she was coping with the whole magic revelation better than I would have if I'd just been tossed into it after that many years. Her personality meshed with Jax's perfectly, the two of them laughing like they'd known each other for years within an hour of him getting to my house this morning.

She continued to practice her magic, no matter how terrified of it she was, only wavering when she came close to hurting me. I'd let her singe me a million times over to see the look she wore last night, the pride on her face when she hit the target in one solid stream of fire. Her eyes lit up, immediately looking to mine as shock consumed her features. I'd leaned against a tree to the left of the target, watching her jump in circles, her dark curls bouncing with the movement as she shrieked and squealed while the target went up in flames.

"Radley?"

"She's talking to you, Romeo." Jax snapped his fingers in front of my face. I batted them away and cleared away the memories of this morning.

"What?" I asked.

Cairo had a grin on her face as she spoke. "I asked what the plan is for today?"

"We could go back to the archives, check out some of the books they have on the town's founding. Might be something in there that can help."

"Boring." Jax coughed the word into his fist.

"Something to add, Jaxy?"

"I was thinking we could see if Torch here has any other Variances. If she managed that," he gestured at my wrist with his fork, "Then odds are flames are the least of what she can do."

Cairo's face paled. Jax had taken to calling her "Torch" after I filled him in on her little fire incident, and I was afraid the nickname was going to stick.

"I don't know about that. I don't think I was really supposed to be able to do that, and that was an accident. I'm a little hesitant to see what comes out when I intentionally push that kind of magic."

"That's fair, but you two are…bonded, right?"

"Right."

"So theoretically, Radley should be able to help temper the flow of magic coming from you."

I looked at him incredulously. "How on earth do you know that?"

"It was in the books you made me find after you two went to the archives. Granted, they're all pretty much fairytales, but there's obviously some truth in there." He shrugged.

"It's worth a shot."

"How do we even practice that? I have no clue what I did back then to call on it, whatever," Cairo waved her hand in the air languidly, panto-miming a gesture of summoning.

"Like any other magic, I would think. We'll try to pull on it and see if it responds."

"It just needs to stay between us three, for now. Just to be safe." I added.

Cairo nodded, nerves making her leg bounce as we finished our break-fast before heading to the backyard. I led her to the middle of the open yard, far enough from the house that it was hopefully out of her range in case she lost control.

"Focus on me. Think about the bond, see if you can feel anything."

She closed her eyes tight, her brows drawn in concentration.

Jax stood to our left, far enough away that he would have time to deflect any misfires, but close enough to intervene if we needed him.

It was early afternoon, and the weather was warm for the time of year. Sweat dotted Cairo's forehead as she pulled on her magic, sifting through to find the bond and the unknown magic that lay beneath it.

"I don't feel anything else, just the fire."

"Dig deeper. When you find what you think is the bottom, push harder."

She closed her eyes once again, focusing intently.

The minutes ticked by, frustration rolling off of her in waves before she let out a small gasp.

A tingle started on my wrist, faint at first, but growing by the second.

"Keep doing whatever you're doing, I can feel it," I called to her.

A gust of shimmering black fog billowed out of her outstretched palms, the strength of it kicking up the leaves on the ground and blowing them around us.

All three of us stood in the middle of the shadow cyclone Cairo had created, our eyes blown wide at the sight of it.

It was massive.

I watched as she took a deep breath, spreading her arms a little farther and tilting her head back, eyes closed, before engulfing the entire area in shadows.

I reached for her, placing one hand cautiously on her waist. The second our bodies made contact, my vision cleared. I was still inside of her shadows, but I could see straight through them. Jax stood with his hands locked behind his neck, a bewildered look on his face as he searched through the shifting darkness with wide eyes.

"Okay, now pull back, Cai," I whispered.

She didn't respond, the shadows instead growing in intensity and swirling around us faster.

"Cairo," I said a little more firmly. "Come on, sweetheart. Pull back."

The fog retracted into her hands like a vacuum, sucking the darkness out of the clearing and allowing the sunlight to stream through again.

Leaves floated down from above our heads and settled back into their piles at our feet. Cairo slumped, her shoulders slouching forward as she closed her eyes and drew a deep breath.

"I-I've nev-I..." I'd never seen Jax speechless before in my life.

"What the fuck was that?" Jax gasped.

A fucking void. The word bounced around my head on repeat.

"I think I found it."

"Yeah, I think you did," I agreed in utter awe.

"There was...more there. It's like there are layers to it, I only pulled on one," she admitted, her voice soft and unsure

Jax let out a string of curses, dragging his hands down the sides of his face. "Dude, we are not equipped to handle this."

He wasn't wrong. But the thought of bringing someone else in to try and help navigate this didn't sound like a good idea. "No one else can know. Besides, it doesn't affect me when I'm touching her," I told him.

Jax furrowed his brows in confusion. "What?"

"I put my hand on her waist, and my vision cleared. The smoke was still there, but I could see through it."

"The bond?"

I nodded.

There was so much we didn't know yet, so much we still had to figure out. But with powers like this, we were for sure on our own here. We couldn't risk the wrong person figuring it out. We couldn't trust anyone for help.

We'd have to do it on our own.

I shook my head in disbelief. "I think I need a drink."

CHAPTER 22:

CAIRO

We entered the small bar and waded through a crowd of people to a booth in the back corner. Music boomed over the speakers, barely covering the sound of pool balls clacking together from the tables to our left. A waitress walked past us carrying a large silver tray filled with plastic shot glasses.

"Shots?" Jax asked, snatching three of them off of the tray.

"Shots," I agreed. Radley looked between the two of us and shook his head.

"I'll grab us some beers."

Radley walked over to the bar to order our drinks, which left me alone at the table with Jax, who had been watching me fiddle with the empty shot glass like it held the answers to the universe.

"You're quiet," he mused, leaning back with a grin. "What are you scheming?"

"Nothing." I laughed. "For tonight, I think I'd just like to have a normal evening."

He hummed in agreement, his eyes sparkling like he'd just thought of the best idea in the world. "You know what you need?"

"More alcohol?"

"Well, yeah. But also—" Before I could stop him, he stood and grabbed my hand, yanking me to my feet.

"Jax, no—"

"Jax, yes!" he said, dragging me toward the center of the bar.

The dance floor wasn't much more than a square of worn wood surrounded by tables, but a few couples were grinding against each other to the song that was blaring around us.

Jax, of course, had no intention of blending in.

He stopped dead in the middle of the floor, turned to me, and bowed

"Shall we?"

"You're ridiculous."

"Ridiculously charming," he corrected, flipping his nonexistent long hair over his shoulder.

I rolled my eyes but took his hand. "You're going to regret this."

"Oh, I already do."

He started twirling me immediately, spinning me around like we were in a ballroom instead of a dive bar. After the fourth spin, I stumbled, grabbing his shoulder for balance.

"Jax!"

"What? You said you wanted fun!" He dropped my hand and launched into some kind of shuffle, kicking his feet out like a poorly coordinated scarecrow while his hands jabbed around his face.

I doubled over laughing. "Are you...voguing?"

"Clearly, you've never seen proper dancing," he said, his hands and feet still moving wildly around him.

"Okay, fine. Two can play this game." I threw my hands in the air and spun in a way that was so chaotic I almost tripped over my own feet. "Behold! The flailing wizard!"

I continued twirling dramatically with my hands above my head, nearly smacking Jax in the face.

Jax screeched, dodging my undulating limbs with a mock glare. "Radley! I feel unsafe! Come get your lady friend!"

Radley was back at the table now, holding three beers and watching the spectacle with an expression caught somewhere between exasperation and amusement.

"Nope," he called out. "You're on your own, buddy. You started it."

Jax turned back to me. "He's abandoning me," he said, his voice full of feigned shock.

"We'll have to lure him in," I proposed. Jax nodded, turning to put his back against mine.

We jumped in a circle, shaking our hips in rhythm with the music and taking turns throwing imaginary lassos and fishing lines at Radley and reeling them in. He pinched the bridge of his nose, shaking his head in spite of the smile I saw appearing at the corners of his mouth.

95

I jumped again, landing directly in front of Radley who must have walked over while Jax was facing him.

"You're both insane," he said, but there was a softness in his voice, like he wasn't entirely mad about it.

"Insanely talented," Jax corrected.

"Dance with me," I coaxed.

Radley grabbed my hand, snatching me away from Jax and securing his hands on my hips.

It was the first time since I'd arrived in Hadeon that I didn't feel terrified or worried, just warm with the alcohol buzzing in my system, and comfortable with Radley and Jax in a way I hadn't felt in years, if ever. Radley spun me in a circle, and then swung me out, where Jax snatched my hand and spun me into him with a smile on his face. A laugh burst out of me as the two of them passed me back and forth, around and around in circles.

I spun into Radley's arms where he leaned down to whisper in my ear.

"You're gorgeous." I could feel the flush creeping into my cheeks and hoped the dim light of the bar would cover it.

He spun me back out to Jax who caught me and leaned in to whisper something of his own.

"You're drooling." He shot me a wink and spun me back out.

I landed against Radley's chest, a giggle bubbling out of me as I stared up at him.

He leaned in closer, his lips so close to mine I could already feel them on me. I decided to blame the alcohol for the way I pushed up on my toes and touched my lips to his in a hesitant kiss. He pulled me closer against him, kissing me back with an equal amount of caution.

The song came to an end as we parted, a lazy smile on his face and a bright red blush certainly on mine.

"Remind me to take you out more," he whispered, his voice as tender as his fingers as they pushed wayward strands of my hair behind my ear.

"You like me buzzed, huh?" I couldn't even remember the last time I had drunk alcohol. College maybe? My tolerance was non-existent, which was currently working in my favor.

"I like you happy." His eyes tracked mine, the gentleness in them making my breath stutter.

He smiled at me, grabbing my hand and pulling me back to our table. I guzzled down one of the beers Radley had brought over, the cool liquid helping dull the voice in my head telling me I was too bold.

Jax clapped Radley on the shoulder as he slid out of his seat. "Be right back. I gotta piss."

Radley rolled his eyes as Jax disappeared into the crowd toward the bathroom.

"He never quits does he?" I asked, taking a sip of my beer.

"Not if he can help it." He chuckled.

For a moment, the noise of the bar seemed to fade. I glanced at Radley, who was watching the doorway where Jax had disappeared. It was on the tip of my tongue to ask him about the kiss, but something about the look on his face made me pause.

"You okay?" I asked, nudging his arm lightly with mine.

Radley's gaze flicked to me, and he hesitated for just a second before answering. "I've been thinking about something."

"That's concerning," I teased.

He didn't laugh. Instead, he tilted his head, studying me in that way he did when he was about to say something important. "You know, I see it."

"See what?"

"The bond," he said, his voice quiet but certain. "Between us."

My chest tightened, not in a bad way, but in the way it always did when the significance of what connected us became impossible to ignore.

"Oh." It wasn't much of a response, but I wasn't sure what else to say.

He leaned back in his chair, his arms crossed loosely over his chest.

"It's…hard for Jax to get close to people, you know. Really close. He doesn't trust easily. But I see a bond building there too."

I blinked, surprised. Jax always seemed so open, like he didn't have a care in the world.

"Really?"

Radley nodded, his expression thoughtful. "Most people don't bother trying to see past all his jokes and bullshit. But you—" He gave me a pointed look. "You didn't even hesitate. It's like you've known him forever."

I felt a warmth spread through my chest. Jax wasn't just some guy who cracked jokes and made me laugh, he was safe in a way I hadn't realized I needed until now.

"I've never had a brother," I began slowly, "but if I did, I'd like to think he'd be like Jax."

Radley's lips quirked in a small, almost relieved smile. "Yeah. That tracks."

I turned to him, my own smile widening. "What about you, then? Big brother? Protective dad? Cranky uncle?"

Radley snorted. "Try 'long-suffering babysitter.'"

"Aww, play nice," I said, though I couldn't stop laughing.

"Remind me to tell you how we met sometime. I practically bullied him out of the constable's little gang." A sly smile spread across his face.

Jax reappeared, sliding back into his seat. "Miss me?"

Radley raised an eyebrow. "We were just debating whether I'm your babysitter or Cairo's."

"Definitely mine," Jax said without hesitation.

Radley sighed, picking up his beer.

I grinned at Jax, raising my glass. "He loves us, really."

Radley grunted, but the ghost of a smile lingered as the two of them followed my lead and raised their glasses, clinking them together with mine.

***

The cool night air hit me hard as we stumbled out of the bar, the icy wind helping to cool my alcohol-warmed cheeks. Jax draped his arm over my shoulders, leaning just enough to make me wonder if he was drunk or just playing it up, while Radley walked a few steps ahead, moving backward like he owned the empty street. Boozy grins rested on both of their faces as they laughed at something Jax had said.

"You are a lightweight," Jax declared, wagging a finger at me.

Radley nodded. "At least she doesn't have to cling to someone just to walk in a straight line."

"Maybe I just want to love on your girl."

I rolled my eyes at both of them. "Pretty sure you've been walking sideways since your first drink," I whispered to Jax.

"Shh. Don't tell dad," He whispered back, his eyes glazed.

We turned the corner, and my laughter died in my throat.

Standing under the streetlamp was a tall man in some kind of police uniform, his silhouette unnervingly sharp against the yellow glow. He didn't move, just watched us approach, his posture too straight, too rigid. The night suddenly felt colder.

"Well, well," he said, his voice smooth, almost casual, but not quite. His gaze landed on me, lingered, then swept over Radley and Jax like he was cataloging every detail.

"Out a little late, aren't we?"

Jax stepped closer to me, blocking the man's line of sight. "Just a harmless night out, Constable," he answered breezily. "Nothing to worry about." There was only a slight slur to his words.

I barely heard him. A chill crawled up my spine, sharp and insistent, as my magic stirred beneath my skin. It wasn't the gentle hum I felt when Radley was near, but something colder, sharper—a warning. I swallowed hard, trying to ignore it, but my eyes flicked to the man's shadow.

It was wrong. The edges stretched too far, twisting unnaturally across the ground. For a moment, it almost looked like it moved on its own.

My breath caught, and I tore my eyes away before anyone noticed.

"Cairo, right?" The constable asked suddenly, and my chest tightened. The way he said my name felt like a hook catching in my ribs. "I've heard about you." His attention was locked on me now, and his voice softened, curious. "I don't believe we've had the chance to talk yet. I'm Vance, but everyone around her refers to me as the constable."

"Nope, I haven't been here long."

"Well, I'm sure I'll be seeing you around."

Radley's hand reached out and found mine, clutching it tightly as he steered me away.

Jax tipped an imaginary hat as we walked past. "Nice seeing you, Constable Buzzkill."

We turned the corner, leaving the man behind, though I could still feel his gaze creeping over my body. Only when we were out of sight did I exhale, my hands trembling.

"What the hell was that?" I whispered.

Radley's grip on my hand tightened. "Nothing good."

"We'll keep an eye on it, Cairo. Don't worry," Jax said, all traces of the lighthearted boy gone from his face and replaced with a seriousness that unnerved me.

I shot him a grateful look, even as I tried to keep my breathing steady. Something about that man was…wrong. I could feel it. And something about the look in his eyes told me he could feel something about me too.

CHAPTER 23:

RADLEY

The bell over the door chimed as I entered the shop, and the smell of dried herbs was equally overwhelming and comforting as I breathed it in. I had spent so much time in this shop growing up. Before I was hanging around to run off the shit heads, I used to come here after school and do my homework at the counter until Mom got off work. It had been a second home for years.

Cheris sat behind the counter, her gray hair pinned up on top of her head and a steaming mug in her hands. Her eyes flicked up, one brow lifting when she saw me.

"Radley," she said, setting the mug down. "Back so soon?" Her voice was calm, but there was a hint of amusement there. She knew I'd be back in her shop.

I leaned against the counter, drumming my fingers against its surface. "Just checking to make sure the goons aren't giving you any trouble lately. It's been kind of quiet."

"Well don't jinx it, you brat," she chastised me, swatting at my arm as she spoke. "That's not all you came in for though, is it? Out with it."

I sighed. There was no fooling that woman, ever. She probably read me the second I walked in.

"I need a favor."

Her expression didn't change, her fingers slowly tracing the rim of her mug as she measured me with her eyes.

"A favor," she repeated. "That's dangerous territory. What kind of favor?"

"I need you to do a reading. For Cairo."

Her eyes narrowed slightly. "The girl you brought in the other day? She's stirred up quite a buzz around here."

I stiffened, trying to play off my reaction with a shrug.

"You know how people around here gossip. She's got questions, and your readings tend to produce answers."

Cheris didn't reply right away. She picked her mug up again, taking a slow sip as she studied my face. "Well, where is she then?"

"We can't do it here. We'll need you to come to my house, where we can be more…discreet about it."

Her lips curved into a slight smile.

"Discretion isn't free, Radley. What's so important that you can't risk walking the girl through my door like everyone else?

I hesitated, quickly scanning the shop to ensure we were alone before leaning forward slightly and dropping my voice low.

"We think she's connected to the prophecy. And we need to figure out who wrote it."

All traces of humor drained from Cheris's face. She set her mug down with deliberate care. "The prophecy," she echoed. "You're not playing with small things, are you?"

I shook my head. "Unfortunately not."

She huffed out a short breath, brushing the hair out of her face.

"Cheris, do you know anything about it? The prophecy, I mean."

For a long moment, she didn't reply. Instead, she slowly stood and moved around the counter, pulling a tin of dried leaves from a nearby shelf. When she opened the lid, the faint aroma of lavender and something citrusy wafted into the air.

"I'll come," she said finally. "But you should know something, Radley."

"What's that?" I asked, my shoulders relaxing slightly.

"When I brew the tea," she said, turning to face me, "I see what the drinker sees."

I blinked at her, caught off guard by how easily she'd revealed her Variance.

"I know more about your Cairo than you think." Her voice was calm but firm. "When you two came in here, I saw the same things she did."

"Why didn't you say anything?"

"It's not my place to put the pieces together, I'm just here to help guide the guests to them," she answered with a shrug. "That doesn't mean I don't know what the pieces are. I know about the prophecy, but I can't talk about it, Radley. We need to leave it at that."

"But you know why this is important?"

"I do," she said softly. "And that's why I will help. But you better make sure Cairo is ready for what she might learn."

"She will be. We don't have a choice."

Cheris gave me a long, searching look before nodding, seeming to be pleased with whatever she found.

"All right. I'll come by tonight after I close up here. But if this backfires, don't blame me."

"Cheris, if this backfires, I don't think we'll be around to place blame on anyone."

***

I pushed open the gate leading to my backyard, following the sounds of laughter and the faint crackle of lingering magic that hovered over the area.

I walked a few steps toward the noise before I stopped, leaning against the side of the house and taking in the scene before me.

Cairo stood in the middle of the open yard, a streak of soot across her cheek and more smudged on her clothes. Her hair was wild, a halo of loose waves that caught the late afternoon light. But the most important thing, the thing that had rooted me to the spot, was the grin on her face. A real, genuine smile spread wide on her face as she raised her hands toward Jax.

The smell of scorched grass drifted over to me where I stood, and I studied the charred ground with a smirk. She was practicing.

"You missed. That was supposed to hit me, right?" Jax said, doubled over as he laughed in between words. "Or was it the dirt's turn for an ass-whooping?"

Cairo bent down, grabbing a clump of singed grass and chucking it at him.

"You keep talking and I'll aim for your face next time."

"You would risk damaging the money maker?" he asked, gesturing wildly at his face.

"Honey, your face was already a lost cause," Cairo retorted, her voice thick with laughter.

"A million dollars says I can hit that oversized ego of yours, though."

She thrust her hands forward, a spark of firing leaping from her fingertips and landing close enough to Jax's pants that he bolted behind the nearest tree.

"Oh look, I got it!" She cackled.

"I yield!" he yelled, still hidden behind the base of a large oak tree.

Cairo tipped her head back, a wave of laughter tumbling out as she wiped tears from her eyes, further smearing the soot that covered her cheeks.

A chuckle slipped out of me, causing Jax to peek his head out from behind the tree as Cairo turned with her hands on her hips.

"Aww, busted. Dad's home," Jax said.

Cairo snorted, wrangling her hair into a loose ponytail and wiping her hands on her pants as I walked toward them.

"I see you two have been busy." I raised an eyebrow at the mess they'd made of the yard.

"I told her she could tear the yard up."

"Generous," I replied dryly. "Did you show her anything useful?"

"Oh yeah, tons of stuff."

I hummed, taking slow steps toward them until I stood a few feet from Jax.

"Did you show her this?"

I flung my hand out, sending a wave of air toward him that knocked him off his feet before pouncing on top of him and lightly boxing at his ribs.

"You prick." He grunted, his hands held tightly to the ground with my magic.

"Language, Jaxy-boy." I laughed, letting out a grunt of my own and falling forward as he burned through my magic and his elbow connected with my side. I rolled off of him, lying on the ground next to his sprawled out body as Cairo stood above us with a smile on her face.

"Alright, ladies. Enough," she said, her eyes brighter than I had seen them since she'd arrived in town.

We stood and brushed ourselves off, though it wasn't doing much for Jax who had grass clumps clinging to the fabric of his clothes.

I looked between the two of them. "Are you two done for the day?"

"Yeah, I think I've had enough for now." Jax shook his head, wiping at the dirt on the back of his neck.

"Good. Now, don't you have a shower waiting for you somewhere that isn't my house?"

"Subtle, as always," Jax said, giving me a salute before heading for the gate.

"I'm out. Try not to set him on fire, okay?"

"No promises," Cairo called after him.

The gate clicked shut, and I turned back to Cairo, watching her brush her hands uselessly against her pants in an effort to remove the black stains from her palms.

Her grin had softened into something smaller, something more private. She looked down at her hands, flexing her fingers.

"Still sinking in, huh?" I asked, stepping closer.

She nodded, biting her bottom lip. "Yeah, I mean I've always felt a little different, but this? I never could have imagined this. Two weeks ago, I didn't even know any of this existed."

She shook her head. "It's terrifying. But, kind of amazing at the same time."

"You are amazing. Even if you look like you just fought a chimney sweep."

She rolled her eyes, but that smile stayed firmly in place.

"Speaking of, I should probably clean up before I ruin your couch."

"Come on, I'll help."

CHAPTER 24:
CAIRO

I followed Radley upstairs, my boots leaving a trail of dark footprints across the floor. I cringed, but he hadn't seemed to notice. He hadn't said much since we left the yard, but I could feel the concern emanating from him—not the sharp, annoyed kind, but the quiet, focused energy that made my heart beat faster.

When we reached the bathroom, he flipped on the light and grabbed a towel from the cabinet, tossing it to me. "Here," he said, leaning against the doorframe. "Start with that before you destroy my entire plumbing system."

I caught the towel and grinned. "Relax. Your shower can't be worse off than the yard."

He gave me a pointed look but didn't reply, his arms crossing over his chest as I turned to the mirror. I winced at the sight. Black streaked my cheeks, my neck, even my hairline. I rubbed at my face with the towel, but it only smeared the mess further.

"Shit," I muttered. "I don't think this is going to cut it. We're going to need a sandblaster."

Radley stepped forward, his voice quieter now. "Hold still, let me try before we bring out the industrial equipment"

Before I could ask what he was doing, he reached out, his hand cupping my chin as his thumb brushed over my cheekbone. The heat of his touch made me freeze.

"You missed a spot," he teased, his smirk stealing my attention over his barely audible words.

"I missed a lot of spots," I murmured, my gaze locked on his.

He didn't answer, dragging his thumb along my jawline, then across my bottom lip. The motion was slow, deliberate. Teasing. My breath hitched, and before I could stop myself, I bit down lightly on the pad of his thumb.

Radley stilled, his eyes darkening as his gaze flicked to my mouth.

"Careful," he warned, his voice dropping lower.

My lips curved into a smirk around his thumb before I let go, stepping back just enough to grab the hem of my shirt. "I thought you weren't afraid of a little dirt," I said, pulling it off in one swift motion and tossing it to the side.

Radley's jaw tightened, but his eyes never left mine.

"Fear is not the emotion I'm experiencing right now, Cairo."

I turned and walked to the shower, feeling the weight of his stare the whole way. I reached for the knob, turning on the water, letting the steam fill the small space. Then glanced over my shoulder, meeting his gaze again. I didn't say anything, I didn't need to. The invitation was clear.

Radley didn't move right away. His hand came up to rub over his jaw, his tension visible in the set of his shoulders.

"You're playing a dangerous game, sweetheart," he said finally, his voice a mix of warning and something else entirely.

"Maybe," I replied, turning back to the water. I quickly stepped out of my pants, kicking them away as I moved my hands deliberately up to my bra.. His eyes tracked me as I unclasped it, letting it hit the floor before turning and stepping under the spray. The heat hit my skin, washing away the soot and grime, leaving only the faint shimmer of magic that always seemed to linger. "But you're still standing there."

The sound of his quiet laugh mixed with the water, and I smiled, letting the warmth of the water wash away the dirt and nerves. I wasn't usually so brazen, but I had felt a pull to Radley since he showed up in my motel room, and every day that feeling grew until it consumed me.

For the first time in weeks, I felt like I could breathe. The chaos of the power, the burden of the prophecy, the questions we didn't have answers to—it all faded for a moment. I was just here, with him, and somehow, that was enough.

I felt his presence behind me a second before I felt his hands settle on my waist, the rough calluses of his palms making my pulse jump. I turned, his hands staying in place as I did and pulling me flush against his body as I faced him. He had stripped completely naked, every inch of his body on display in front of me.

He ran a finger over the mess on my neck.

"Was this just a ploy to get me naked?" he asked wryly.

"You caught me. I had to get Jax to toss me into a campfire."

"Smartass." He smiled, that million dollar smile that I only saw in the quiet moments when it was just the two of us.

His green eyes pierced into me, strands of black hair falling over his forehead as he looked down at me.

"You're doing so well, Cai. With how new all of this is for you, it's amazing watching you absorb and own every bit of it."

"I'm trying. It helps, having you."

His eyes bounced between mine, searching for something I hoped he found. His hands tightened on my waist, drawing a soft gasp from my lips that had his eyes flying wide.

"Cairo, if you don't want this, tell me."

"What if I do want it?"

"Then tell me you do, because I'm holding your wet, naked body in my hands, and I'm about to lose my fucking mind."

"I want you, Radley."

That was all he needed to hear. His mouth descended on mine, a delicious desperation in the way he consumed me with his kiss. He traced the seam of my lips with his tongue, begging for entrance, and I obliged, circling his tongue with mine and savoring the taste of him as he explored my mouth.

One hand came up and threaded through the hair at the base of my neck, tipping my head back for better access as he took the kiss deeper, each stroke of his tongue feeding the fire growing in my belly.

He bit gently into my bottom lip before soothing the sting with his tongue, prompting an involuntary moan to escape me, followed by a deep groan from his throat.

Both of his hands slipped under my thighs, the callouses on his fingers rough against my skin as he lifted me. He took two steps to the shower wall and braced me against it, settling between my thighs while his mouth found my neck.

"You are the most beautiful creature I have ever seen." His words were muffled against my skin, his lips trailing kisses down my neck and over my chest.

My cheeks heated under his praise, the soft touch of his lips a stark contrast to the way his fingers were digging into my thighs.

"I want to taste every inch of your body."

He trailed lower, dipping his head to take one of my nipples in his mouth and flick his tongue around it in circles. My head met the shower wall as I threw it back, clenching my jaw at the bolts of pleasure that traveled from the bud in his mouth and landed somewhere below my belly button.

He raised his head to look at me, his green eyes meeting mine in the steamy shower as he knelt on the floor at my feet, carefully lifting one of my legs and resting my foot on his knee.

His warm hands skimmed up my calf, massaging as he moved higher, before placing his hand under my knee and lifting my leg over his shoulder, giving him unrestricted access to my aching core.

The vulnerability had me squeezing my legs closed, but his gentle hands stopped them from touching.

"Don't hide from me, Cai. There is no part of you that I don't want to worship. Let me have this?"

His voice was wary, questioning.

He's asking permission to worship me? Fuck, I think I already came.

I nodded, my bottom lip tucked between my teeth, and he dipped his head between my legs.

The first swipe of his hot tongue against my center had my hips rolling forward of their own accord, chasing the pleasure he promised with each swirl of his tongue against me.

His hands came to rest on my hips, pulling me firmly against his mouth and locking me in place as he set a brutal pace of sucking and licking that made my thighs tremble on either side of his head.

I twined my fingers in his hair, pushing and pulling as the pleasure built toward release.

"Radley." His name was a whisper, a breath on my lips as he pushed me closer to the edge.

He groaned into me in answer, the vibration from his mouth adding to the fire he was stoking.

He pulled back, raising two fingers to his lips and slipping them into his mouth before pulling them out and placing a soft kiss just above my clit. My pulse skittered across my neck as he reached between my thighs, dragging his fingers through my slick core before slowly pushing both digits into me. I sucked in a sharp breath at the overwhelming sensation, the sound muffled by the falling water of the showerhead beside us as he began pumping them in and out at a torturous rhythm.

My muscles tightened with every twist of his wrist, his fingers curling up in a perfect arch to hit a spot inside me I hadn't known existed until this moment. Every thrust of his fingers coiled me tighter until I felt like I was going to explode. Beads of sweat gathered between my breasts, running down the planes of my stomach as I gripped his hair tighter, bracing for the impact of what he was building.

He leaned in, flicking his tongue in tight circles over my clit, until I couldn't take it anymore and I finally came undone. I slammed my eyes shut reflexively as my cries echoed off of the glass doors of the shower, my nails digging into his scalp as I tried to focus on the praise tumbling from his lips.

"Fucking gorgeous, baby."

He moved my leg off his shoulder, standing slowly and leaning in to place a kiss on my forehead.

"Let's get you cleaned up, and we'll finish this somewhere dry."

It was all I could do to nod through the aftershocks.

CHAPTER 25:

RADLEY

We had just exited the bathroom when the doorbell rang. I muttered a curse under my breath as I threw on a pair of sweats and gave Cairo a pleading look.

"We have to let her in, we can finish this later," she whispered, pulling a sweatshirt over her head and digging around in the dresser for a pair of shorts.

I closed my eyes, praying to any god that was listening for a soft dick and an inordinate amount of patience, and then went down the stairs to open the door.

Cheris stood on the front porch, looking displeased at the sight of my shirtless torso. She stepped into the house, glancing around with the practiced ease of someone who saw too much but rarely commented.

"Nice place," she said lightly, though her sharp eyes were already scanning the room, landing briefly on me, then Cairo. "Feels…lived in."

"For fucks sake," I muttered, earning a sharp look from Cairo as she closed the door behind Cheris.

Cheris smirked, setting down a worn leather satchel on the table. "I don't judge. Shall we get started?"

Years of experience told me that was bullshit. She judged. She judged a lot.

Cairo hesitated, glancing at me. I gave her a slight nod. We didn't have many leads, and whatever Cheris could pull from her tea leaves was better than nothing. Cheris busied herself preparing the tea. She moved with ease, her hands steady as she poured the boiling water and her demeanor calm despite the strained atmosphere. At this point, brewing tea had to be muscle memory for her. For as long as I could remember, Cheris had owned that shop and probably went through ten pots a day, catering to whatever need her clients had with a warm cup of steeped herbs.

When she finally handed Cairo the steaming cup, her voice softened. "Drink slowly. Focus on what you're looking for."

Cairo's fingers trembled slightly as she took the cup, her gaze flicking between me and Cheris before settling on the swirling surface of the tea. She sipped, her brow furrowed in concentration.

Cheris closed her eyes, her hands resting on the table, and for a long moment, the room was silent except for the faint creak of the house settling.

Then her eyes snapped open, and I saw something flash in them— something ancient and heavy, like she'd glimpsed a piece of the past no one was supposed to see.

"What is it?" I asked, my voice harsher than I intended.

Cheris didn't answer right away. She stared at Cairo, her expression unreadable, before finally looking down at the cup Cairo had set on the table. She turned it slowly, her fingers brushing over the rim as she studied the patterns left behind.

"Your mother," Cheris said to Cairo quietly, "made a bargain to save you. A bargain with something old. Older than this town, older than anything you could imagine."

Cairo stiffened beside me. "What kind of bargain?"

Cheris didn't look up. "To protect you from someone—or something—chasing her. She gave up something precious in return."

"What was she running from?" I pressed.

Cheris's gaze darted to me, sharp and cautious. "Something dark. Something powerful. But whatever it was, she was desperate enough to make a deal with…" She paused, her fingers brushing the surface of the table as if weighing her words.

"With what?" Cairo's voice was barely above a whisper.

Cheris sighed, leaning back in her chair. "An ancient being. One who doesn't give without taking in return. But they kept their word—your mother and you were hidden, and everyone forgot you."

Everyone except me, I thought, though I didn't say it out loud.

Cairo leaned forward, her hands gripping the edge of the table. "Who is this being? Where do I find them?"

Cheris stood, gathering her satchel with deliberate slowness. "Be careful what you wish for, Cairo."

"Cheris," I said, my voice low. "If you know something, say it."

She hesitated at the door, her hand resting on the handle. "You'll find them at the ruins outside of town. But tread carefully. They don't give answers freely, and they always take more than you think you're offering."

She took a single step, then turned back around, digging through her bag until she pulled out an aged piece of paper. She thrust it toward me, placing it in my hand and then covering it with her own.

"I can't tell you everything you need to know, Radley. I wish I could. Take this, and find out what you can about the Obsidian Caves on the outskirts of town. I only saw a flash, so don't ask me why, just look into it."

I studied her face, the tightness around her eyes and the pinch of her mouth telling me she was holding her tongue.

"Alright. Thank you, Cheris."

She nodded, and with that, she was gone, leaving Cairo and me sitting in the heavy silence of the aftermath.

"What do we do now?" she asked, her voice small in the empty room.

"We do what we can to prepare, and then we go to the ruins."

CHAPTER 26:

CAIRO

My stomach churned with uneasiness as I fought with my hair, wrangling it into a clip at the back of my head and pulling on a sweater. I needed time to process everything that had happened since I left my father's house—Radley, the magic, the secrets my mother was keeping. But there was no time; there wasn't an opportunity to have a breakdown when we were constantly in a race to put the pieces of this puzzle together. I clutched my mother's necklace in my hands, squeezing my eyes shut and begging for guidance. I missed her more now than I ever had. In the midst of everything going on, I just wanted to hear her voice. She would be able to explain so much of this, but she wasn't here. I had to find answers for myself.

The ruins lay at the north end of Hadeon, down what felt like a never-ending path through the dense woods that seemed to suck the sunlight from the sky. The closer we got, the darker everything felt, like the world itself was holding its breath, waiting for something precious to shatter.

Radley was driving, leaving me to try and wrap my head around Cheris's revelations as I sat in the passenger seat with my head resting against the window.

The prophecy.

The bargain.

The ever-growing power inside me.

It was all too much to process at once. My chest ached from the weight of it all, a knot tightening every time I tried to draw a full breath.

"You're quiet," Radley said, his voice breaking through the hum of the engine. His eyes flicked toward me, dark and searching before settling back on the road.

"Do you think it's true?" I asked apprehensively.

Radley didn't pretend to not know what I meant. He tapped the steering wheel with his fingers, his brow furrowed in thought.

"I think prophecies are like maps," he answered finally. "Useful if you know where you're going, but they don't show you every bend in the road. They don't decide which path you take. You do."

"That's…surprisingly wise, Mr. Cordova."

"Don't get used to it."

We fell quiet again, but his words stuck with me. The idea that I wasn't just a pawn in some ancient game, that maybe—just maybe—I still had a choice gave me a sense of comfort I desperately needed.

The ruins came into view just as twilight began to creep over the landscape. They weren't much to look at, honestly, just a cluster of jagged stones rising out of the earth like broken teeth.

But as we drew closer, I felt it.

Power. Old and restless. It pressed against my skin like static, making the hair on my arms stand on end.

Radley pulled the car to a stop at the edge of the ruins, cutting the engine.

"You feel it?" he asked, glancing at me.

"Yeah," I whispered. "It's…loud."

He nodded, unbuckling his seatbelt and grabbing the bag of supplies from the backseat.

"Stay close," he said, his voice firm.

I slid out of the car, the cool air brushing against my warm skin. The ruins loomed ahead, and for a moment, I hesitated.

Radley stood beside me, his hand brushing mine briefly as if to ground me. "You sure about this?"

I nodded, though my stomach twisted with nerves. I wasn't sure. Not really. But we had no choice. "It's the only way."

I unfolded the paper Cheris had given Radley last night. The ritual was simple enough in theory: a circle of salt and dried herbs we got from Cheris, a candle lit with magic, and the offering of something meaningful. My mother's necklace—the one tangible connection I had to her—rested in the center of the circle. Its metallic gleam caught the dying light.

"It's just a trinket," I said softly, trying to convince myself it wasn't a big deal.

Radley gave me a sweet smile. "It's more than that. That's what makes it work."

I gave him a half-hearted nod, but his words calmed me.

I knelt and lit the candle, my magic sparking to life with a faint sizzle of black smoke. As the flame caught, the air shifted and the ruins around us groaned like they were alive.

Radley crouched beside me, his voice low. "Whatever happens, I'm right here with you."

I didn't have time to respond before the candle flickered violently, and the shadows around us seemed to thicken, spiraling toward the center of the circle. My stomach clenched as a cold wind surged through the ruins, carrying with it a sound that wasn't quite a voice but wasn't quite silence either.

They had arrived.

It didn't take a distinct shape at first, just a swirling mass of shadow and light, the air around us rippling with its presence. When it finally spoke, its voice was everywhere and nowhere at once.

"Who calls me?"

Radley tensed beside me, his hand brushing my shoulder. "Go ahead," he murmured.

I swallowed hard, my voice trembling. "Cairo Hallivand. What is your name?"

"Nytheris," the voice answered, the words coming out somewhere between a purr and a hiss.

I cleared my throat, willing it to come out stronger. "Nytheris, we need answers. About my magic. About the deal my mother made."

The shadows shifted, forming the vague outline of a humanoid figure.

"You demand much," it replied, its tone almost amused. "And offer little."

Radley straightened, his jaw tight. "She doesn't demand. She asks. Respectfully."

The figure turned toward him, its formless face tilting as though studying him. "And you," it said, voice dropping to a deeper, more sinister tone, "are her tether. Curious."

Radley didn't flinch. "Yes."

The being laughed, the sound a low rumble that seemed to shake the earth beneath us.

"Arrogant. Protective. Foolish." Its focus shifted back to me. "Show me then, how you tether an untamable magic."

I reached for Radley's hand, and he took it eagerly. As soon as our palms touched, my magic surged, darker and wilder than ever before. The shadows that had been swirling around the being now turned inward, drawn toward us.

Radley's grip tightened. "I've got you. Just focus."

The energy inside me built, every cell in my body vibrating with the oncoming of a storm I couldn't contain. I gasped as the being's voice thundered around us. "He stabilizes you. He grounds you. But the price of such devotion is high."

Radley gritted his teeth. "Save the lecture."

"If he does not let go, he will die," Nytheris warned, its voice echoing around us as it spoke. "His body cannot withstand your power."

I froze, panic gripping me. "Radley—"

"I accept the risk," he cut me off, conviction clear in his words. He wasn't going to leave, even if staying meant putting himself in danger.

His hand in mine was steady and unrelenting.

The being seemed to loom closer, its shadowy form expanding. "You would give your life for her?"

"Yes," Radley answered without hesitation.

My breath hitched. "Radley, don't—"

"I've made my choice," he said firmly, his eyes locking on mine. "Focus, Cairo."

The being was silent for a long, excruciating moment, the tension crackling like lightning in the air. Then it laughed again, the sound vibrating through my bones.

I gritted my teeth against the fire that raced under my skin.

"Enough," the voice demanded.

I took a deep breath, bending forward as the magic around us funneled back into my outstretched palm.

"Interesting," it said. "Your bond is strong. That will come in handy later."

The gloomy figure leaned closer to me, and the air grew colder. "You are the daughter of prophecy, Cairo. Your power was destined to be the key to a new age. But someone has tainted that destiny—warped it for their own purpose."

My heart pounded. "Who?"

The being's voice echoed with finality. "You will not find the answer here. Look inward, you already know his name, hmm?" There was a smugness in the words, a sense that it knew exactly what I wanted to hear, but was going to force us to do the leg work ourselves.

I barely managed to nod, my body trembling from the strain of holding my magic. The being turned back to Radley. "The bond between you exists because I allowed it. Gifted it. You are the only thing standing between her and her death. Remember that."

And just like that, the shadows dispersed, leaving us alone in the ruins with nothing but the faint flicker of the candle.

Radley let go of my hand as I collapsed onto my knees, my breath coming in ragged gasps.

He knelt beside me, his face pale but determined.

"You okay?" he asked, his voice soft now.

"You could've died," I whispered, my voice breaking.

"But I didn't." His lips twitched into the hint of a smile.

I let out a shaky exhale, tears stinging my eyes. "You're stubborn."

"And you're alive," he said simply. "That's all that matters."

For a moment, we sat there in the fading light, the ruins around us silent once more.

I stared at my hands, willing the trembling to ease. Maybe it was from the amount of magic I'd used, or the nerves that had formed a tangled heap of dread in my stomach. Maybe both.

"You need to eat," Radley said.

"I don't think I can after that." I huffed out a humorless laugh.

"I know, but you used a fuck ton of energy. Come on," he said, reaching his hand out for mine and leading me back to the car. "Just something small. Okay?"

"Okay." The word tasted like ash as it left my mouth.

CHAPTER 27:

RADLEY

The only diner in town was Molly's. It was the kind of place where the smell of bacon grease had soaked into every surface, and the coffee was always just a little too bitter, but it was also the only place you could get a decent burger.

Cairo slid into the booth across from me, glancing around like the place held some kind of secret.

"It's charming," she said, her voice still holding a slight quiver from the events of the day.

"Never heard anyone call it that before." I laughed, flipping over the laminated menu. Not that I needed to look—I'd ordered the same thing here since I was a kid.

Cairo glanced out the window, her eyes flitting over the handful of people walking by.

"Do you think anyone else knows about…all of this?"

I steepled my hands under my chin as I thought about it

"I honestly couldn't say. I mean, the prophecy I heard about when I was younger, but just as part of the town's history, not as if it was something that was actually pertinent to our lives here. Same with Nytheris. We heard about the gods, but no one here worships them or anything like that. I certainly didn't expect to see one in person."

Before she could respond, a waitress appeared at the table, notepad in hand.

"Radley, same as always?" she asked

"Yes, please." She gave me a quick nod before turning to Cairo.

Cairo gave her a polite smile. "I'll have the same as him."

The waitress lingered just a little too long, curiosity practically radiating off her as she studied Cairo's face, before finally speaking quietly.

"Is Jax joining you?" The rosy tint to her cheeks told me she was hoping I would say yes. Her fingers fiddled nervously with the notepad in her hands as she looked everywhere except our faces and waited for a response.

"No, not today."

"Oh, okay. That's fine, I was just-for the order. You know," she stammered, turning and walking away at a clipped pace.

Cairo leaned forward, her voice low. "What was that about?"

"I think she's secretly in love with him," I said, smirking. "And he somehow hasn't picked up on it yet."

Her laugh was soft but genuine, and for a second it felt like the diner had faded into the background.

"Radley!"

The sharp voice pulled me out of the moment, and my stomach lurched. I turned to see my mom standing by the counter, a to-go coffee cup in her hand, her eyes already locked on us.

"Hey, mom," I replied, leaning back in the booth as she made her way over.

"Hello, my boy." She moved her gaze from me to Cairo. "Cairo. Right?" she asked.

"Yes ma'am, we met a few days ago."

"Of course. Nice to see you again, honey." I watched as her eyebrows drew together, her lips pursing slightly as she stared at Cairo's face.

"Mom?"

"Sorry," she said, looking to me and then immediately back to Cairo. "You just look so familiar." Mom ran her fingers over her lips as she mumbled under her breath. "Cairo…" The word was just a whisper.

"I think I just have one of those faces," Cairo joked nervously, her eyes darting to me full of questions.

"No, that's not it. You-you look like——" She stopped before she finished her sentence, seeming to snap out of a trance as she suddenly straightened and lightly shook her head.

"Well, I better be getting home. Come by the house soon, honey. I'll fix dinner for you." She patted my shoulder and offered a small wave to Cairo before heading toward the door and exiting the diner.

"What the hell was that about?"

"I think…she might be remembering you. Or your name, maybe."

"That's impossible. No one here except you should remember me at all." Cairo's voice was quiet, but an edge of panic had seeped in.

"I know, I know."

I scrubbed my hands over my face as we both mulled the interaction over.

How could she remember her? She didn't recognize her the other day when we were at her house, so why now?

How?

A small gasp escaped Cairo's lips, calling my attention back to her.

"Radley…" she started. "The bargain."

"What about it?"

"We had to leave, and stay hidden, right?"

"Right?"

"The price for that was that no one here would remember us, and my mother's magic."

"Correct."

"I came back."

The realization dawned on me, and I felt fucking stupid for not seeing it sooner.

"It's void. The bargain is void, because you came back."

She nodded slowly, resignation on her face.

"So, if my mom is starting to remember you, then whoever was after the two of you before will remember you too."

Cairo rested her head in her hands, strands of her dark hair spilling over her arms as she worried her bottom lip between her teeth, tension causing a line to appear between her brows.

"This is starting to feel like too much, Radley. I don't know what to do or where to start, and everywhere we look there's another threat or another life-altering revelation. I'm going to lose my mind."

"You're not going to lose your mind, Cai. I'll put a leash on it if I need to." I had a maddening desire to chip the weight of the worry off of her shoulders. Who was she when she wasn't drowning in her fate? I knew in that moment that I would do whatever it took to find out.

"Har Har," she fake-laughed in response, the smallest of smiles playing at the corners of her full lips and pulling all of my attention to her mouth, once again.

God she was beautiful.

"I'm serious. I know a lot has happened in the last couple of days, but you aren't alone. And worst case scenario, people start remembering. Your mom was adored in this town. By default, you'll have a lot of people on your side."

She nodded, but I could see the concern in her eyes, the fear and exhaustion that had settled deep in her bones.

I reached across the table, pulling her hand free of her hair and cradling it in mine.

"You're safe with me."

***

The smell of old books and too-strong coffee lingered around the living room as the three of us huddled around my coffee table. Some of the covers were so worn that the titles were illegible, while others were handbound and handwritten bearing no title at all.

Jax was sprawled out on his back to my left, holding a book above his head as he mumbled along with the words under his breath. Cairo sat cross-legged beside me, her bottom lip tucked between her teeth once again as she poured over whatever it was that she was reading.

I reached toward the stack, pulling yet another heavy book out and checking the spine.

"Light and Shadow: A History."

"This one might be something," I said, trying hard to keep any sliver of hope that I had out of my voice so I didn't have to disappoint Cairo if it was another dead end.

We'd been at this for hours, pouring over the prophecy and trying to decipher it, flipping through at least a dozen of the books we'd pulled from my father's old study. So far, we hadn't found anything useful.

"What is it?" Cairo asked, inching closer to me to look over my shoulder.

I showed her the title. "It sounds like what Nytheris was saying, right?"

"So fucking strange to me that you two just casual talked to a god," Jax mused.

"Trust me, it wasn't casual," I quipped before turning my attention back to the book in my hands.

I skimmed the opening lines, my brow furrowing.

"In the beginning, there were two—a star to guide the lost and a shadow to swallow the broken. Their bond created the world, but their discord shattered it."

"Ominous," Jax mumbled.

"Sounds right, though. Keep going," Cairo urged.

"The Star gave life, the Shadow sought control. Their creations were bound to their essence, their power flowing through the veins of the land. But their hearts clashed, and in their fury, the Star wove a prophecy of renewal while the Shadow answered with one of destruction."

"Yup. That's definitely them," Jax said, his voice grim.

I flipped through the pages, finding more scattered mentions of the gods.

"The Star sacrificed herself to bind the Shadow, yet even in chains, his whispers seep into the hearts of men. Beware those who seek his favor, for they will bring ruin masked as salvation."

"Sounds a lot like the constable," Cairo muttered.

I nodded.

"This is good, but it's still pieces. We need something that connects it all. Something that explains where the other prophecy is, and why they're colliding now," I said, closing the book and setting it in my lap.

Jax leaned back, tossing his book back onto the pile. "So what, we keep going until our eyes fall out?"

"There's probably something in the boxes at my mom's house. She packed up some of the stuff from Dad's study when she left, and we haven't looked through any of that yet. He had shelves of old journals and records that she wanted to take with her."

Jax's eyebrows shot up. "You're just now mentioning this?"

"I wasn't convinced we'd find the answers on paper. I've lived here all my life, and no one has ever given Nytheris or Vaelith much thought. They were always just legends."

"You're the worst," Jax groaned, throwing a wadded sheet of paper at me.

"You'll live." I stood, stretching my stiff limbs. "Come on. Let's go see if there's anything in those journals that can help."

Cairo was furiously jotting things down in her notebook as we stood up and walked toward the garage.

We were on the cusp of figuring out the puzzle we'd been placed in. I could feel it.

I had been racking my brain for anything I'd learned about the gods over the years. Nytheris said the bond between Cairo and I existed because she had allowed it, that it was a gift. So Cairo had been a part of this prophecy since at least then. We had no idea if it was the kind of thing she was born into, or if she somehow caught the attention of a god at the ripe old age of eight, and was chosen then. There were dozens more questions than answers, each new bit of information changing the way we had always looked at things here.

If people knew you could summon a god just up the road, how different our lives would be.

The only thing we knew was that the clock was ticking. As soon as this town remembered Cairo and her mom, she would be in more danger than ever before.

We needed to figure out who was after her before that happened.

And I needed to keep her safe.

CHAPTER 28:

CAIRO

Radley unlocked the door with a practiced flick of his wrist, pushing it open and allowing me to pass through, both him and Jax following closely behind.

"Mom?" he called out. "Her car wasn't here. I don't think she's home."

"Good, that saves us from having to lie to her about why we're here," I said.

"I feel like I'm breaking into someone's house to do shady shit," Jax added in a harsh whisper.

I laughed. "You are."

He led us toward a door at the far end of the hallway.

The room was small, boxes piled in the corners. Some of them had been emptied, their contents placed around the room so that it resembled a study. Shelves lined the walls, crammed with books of all sizes, their spines cracked and worn. A large wooden desk sat in the middle of the room, covered in papers, ink pots, and a faded green lamp.

Radley sighed.

"She set it up just like his old office."

The air smelled musty, like old paper and dust. It was obvious no one had spent much time in here; the room seemed frozen in time.

Radley walked over to a tall cabinet against the far wall and pulled it open to reveal more books and folders stuffed full of loose-leaf papers.

"This is where he kept the stuff he didn't want anyone else messing with," he explained.

"Journals, records, things he found or wrote himself." Radley pulled out leather journals bound with string and handed one to me and one to Jax, grabbing a large stack of papers for himself and settling in on the floor by the cabinet.

"Start with these," he said. "Look for anything that mentions the gods, the prophecies, or the town's history."

Jax and I followed suit, making ourselves comfortable on our respective spots on the floor and shuffling through papers, skimming every line. I flipped open the journal in my hands, the pages filled with neat, cramped handwriting.

The entries were dated, some going back over a hundred years. As I scanned them, I caught snippets of information: mentions of the ruins, old rituals, and fleeting references to Nytheris and Vaelith—the darker of the two Gods. They had existed in the same time, neither of them ever landing on the same page when it came to how the human race should be guided. Nytheris cherished balance of power above all else; she firmly believed that no one person should hold more power than the next. Vaelith, on the other hand, believed it was better to have a handful of extraordinarily powerful people than mass amounts of moderately-gifted ones. That was the basis of their feud and ultimately, what took them out.

Jax, of course, broke the silence first.

"Why does your dad's handwriting look like it belongs to a serial killer?" he asked, holding up a page of chicken-scratch words, the writing traveling every direction across the paper.

Radley didn't even look up. "Keep reading, Jax."

"Just saying. It's creepy."

I ignored them, flipping through the pages of the journal I was studying. About halfway through, something caught my eye. An entry dated nearly two centuries ago:

"The two prophecies are like mirrors—each reflecting the other, but one warped, twisted by shadow. The first speaks of renewal and rebirth. The second promises destruction cloaked in power. Both are tied to time, to the celestial cycle, and to those chosen by the gods themselves."

I read the passage aloud, my voice quiet but firm.

Radley frowned, setting his journal down.

"There's our confirmation that there's a second prophecy."

"There's more." I traced my finger over the words as I continued.

"The Shadow's prophecy hides its champion in plain sight, a pawn unaware of its role until it's too late. Beware the one who seeks the power of the gods, for they are the harbinger of the end."

"Champion?" Jax asked, his tone suddenly serious. "Like…a person?"

"That's what it sounds like," I responded, glancing between them. "Someone tied to the second prophecy. Someone who doesn't even know they're involved until it's too late."

Radley's jaw tightened, his expression dark.

"The constable."

"Wait, you think he's the champion?" Jax asked

Radley nodded. "It makes sense. He's been acting strange as fuck for months. Making deals, consolidating power, sending his minions all over town. And if he's tied to this…" he trailed off, the unspoken implications clear.

I swallowed hard, flipping through more pages. "We need to figure out exactly what the second prophecy says. Nytheris said it's hidden somewhere, we just don't know where."

Radley leaned back against the wall, running a hand through his hair. "We'll start with the ruins. If the first prophecy is tied to them, then maybe the second one is, too."

Jax grinned, though it didn't quite reach his eyes.

"Great. More wandering around creepy ruins that are haunted by ancient gods."

Radley shot him a look, but I cut in before they could start arguing.

"Focus, both of you. If the constable is tied to this, we need proof, and we need to figure out who the actual champion is. If it's not him…"

"It could be anyone."

The realization settled over us as we sifted through the journals, searching for more answers. Somewhere in these pages, in the ruins, or in the whispers of the town itself, the truth was waiting for us.

We just had to find it.

***

Radley leaned against the edge of his desk, arms crossed and eyes narrowed at the crow perched on the windowsill. Its head tilted, beady black eyes locking on him like it had secrets to spill. There was something unnerving about the way it stared back at him, a deliberate intensity that made the air around me feel heavy. Jax had gone home to "rest his brain," as he put it, leaving just Radley and me in the study. And his bird.

"Is that…normal?" I asked, motioning toward the bird as it ruffled its feathers.

"For a crow?" Radley smirked, his sharp jaw tightening as if he were amused by some inside joke. "Not exactly."

With a slow exhale, he extended his hand toward the bird. Its beak parted slightly, and a misty shimmer passed between them, like translucent threads weaving some unspoken message. The connection broke as Radley dropped his hand and pushed off the desk, looking smug and entirely too comfortable with the situation.

"You sent it, didn't you?" I accused, suddenly piecing it together. "Back at the motel. That crow—it was you."

His grin turned lazy, wolfish. "I had to be sure."

"Sure of what?" I pressed, crossing my arms over my chest.

Radley's gaze met mine, steady and unflinching. "That it was you. I felt it the second you passed through the veil into Hadeon. This," he said, holding out his wrist to show me the mark, "started … pulsing. It was like a beacon, guiding me to where you were. The bond we share, it's not exactly subtle, Cai."

I blinked at him, letting his words sink in. "You sent a bird to spy on me? You are so creepy sometimes."

He chuckled, low and warm. "Maybe. But I had to know. I couldn't risk it being someone—or something—else."

The crow cawed, and Radley turned back to it, his expression sharpening.

"I use them to keep tabs on the town," he explained. "My magic is a Conduit, it lets me channel power into living things. With the birds, it's simple: I give them a little push, and they bring me back what they see."

"Spies."

"Smart ones," he countered, a trace of pride in his voice. "The constable thinks his grunts are sneaky, but they're nothing compared to a few well-placed crows."

I stepped closer to the bird, its glossy feathers gleaming in the light. "And what did this one see?"

Radley hesitated, his fingers brushing over the crow's head as if drawing the information from it. His face darkened slightly, his smirk fading.

"The constable was in the woods, near the ruins. He's meeting with… I'm not sure.. But whatever it is, it's not human."

The thought sent a shiver down my spine.

"Think he's planning something?"

Radely nodded. "Probably. I'll send more out tonight to keep watch."

The crow let out another sharp caw and I swore it shifted its gaze to me, almost looking judgmental.

"What?" I asked, half-laughing at the absurdity of feeling scrutinized by a bird.

"It's just curious," Radley said, his tone softening. "They can sense the magic in you now, too."

An unpleasant reminder.

"You don't think the constable knows yet, do you?"

"He suspects, I'm sure," he answered. "But he doesn't know what you're capable of. Not yet. That's our advantage, for now."

I leaned against the desk beside him, my shoulder brushing his.

I tilted my head up, my eyes meeting Radley's. The bright green of his irises hadn't become any less shocking since the first time I saw them. The small golden flecks swimming in lime green caught the light and danced with amusement. I noticed the corner of his mouth ticking up.

"See anything you like?" he asked, his voice a low whisper.

"Yes."

He leaned down, his lips hovering an inch from mine.

I closed my eyes, feeling his breath on my lips. Just a little further…

The crow cawed loudly again, as if to scold us for wasting time.

I startled and jumped backward as Radley straightened and let out a chuckle.

"Time to send him back out. We've got work to do."

I watched the crow spread its wings and launch into the sky, disappearing into the fading light.

"I'm going to go check in with Cheris, see if she has any more vague bits of information she wants to bestow upon me. I won't be long," he assured me.

"Okay." I nodded, biting my bottom lip as he reached out, catching one of my stray curls in his hand and rubbing it between his forefinger and thumb as he studied me.

"And Cairo?"

"Yeah?"

"When I get back, I'm finishing that kiss." His words come out so confident, so sure as he glided his fingers down the length of the hair, before letting go and backing out of the room with a smile.

"Okay." I blinked, my cheeks already feeling warm at the promise in his voice.

CHAPTER 29:

RADLEY

I made the short walk to Jax's house, calling down two of the smaller crows that stuck close to me and guiding them into his open window.

Don't hurt him, just make him scream.

I listened closely, the light breeze and rustling leaves across the street the only noise around me until—

"GODDAMNIT!" The frantic flapping of wings mixed with the sound of something that sounded like a stack of books hitting the floor.

That shit never got old.

I let myself in the front door, walking silently up the stairs and following Jax's sounds of panic to his open bedroom door.

He was in the middle of the room, spinning in haphazard circles and flailing his arms. His foot caught one of the books he dropped and sent him sprawling across his bed.

"RADLEY. Call off your birds, dick."

Ease.

The birds perched on his headboard. Their heads tilted in sync with one another as they watched him.

"You good, buddy?"

"You good buddy?" he mimicked, snatching a pillow off his bed and flinging it at my face.

"That trick is so old, dude."

"Still fucks you up, though, doesn't it?" I asked, my smile smug as he stood and brushed himself off.

"You'll get yours, don't worry."

"Just trying to lighten the mood, Jaxy-boy."

He rolled his eyes, shoving me playfully in the chest as we stooped down to pick up the books.

"Are you reading...*smut?*" I laughed at the description on the back cover.

Definitely smut.

"Do not judge." He accentuated his words with a finger jabbed in my direction as he snatched the book out of my hands.

"Hey, no judgment. Curiosity, maybe, but no judgement," I said, raising my hands in front of me.

"No one else home?"

"No." His voice was tight. "They're out. Who fucking knows where."

I nodded. His parents were a touchy subject. Thankfully, they weren't around much. Usually at the bar in town, or sleeping off a hangover at the motel.

I followed Jax out the front door, our steps slow as we made our way back toward my house, cutting through the center of town to shorten the walk.

Something pulled at my gut, a subtle internal warning.

The air felt off.

Everything felt off, actually. The cobblestones under my boots seemed to vibrate faintly with each step.

Jax walked beside me, his shoulders loose and his face relaxed. It took a lot to spook him, but I'd seen it this afternoon. I don't think any of us really grasped the magnitude of everything happening until we saw it in front of us.

I'd been hearing whispers from the crows for days about the constable's little grunts. Trent, Saul, and Mack had been asking about Cairo, which made me uneasy. They would find something out sooner or later.

As we made it to the end of the street, I could see them standing on the corner just outside of Cheris's shop, clustered together like they were waiting for us.

"Don't say it," Jax muttered under his breath.

"I didn't say anything," I replied, keeping my tone low.

"You're thinking it though."

"Maybe."

Trent spotted us first, his eyes narrowing as he elbowed Mack and nodded toward us. They turned in unison, their expressions shifting from surprise to something more smug.

"Well, well. Just the boys we were looking for."

"Did daddy send you after us?" I asked, not breaking stride.

Saul stepped forward. He was all brawn and no brain.

"You've been doing an awful lot of research, Radley. Anything in particular caught your interest?"

I folded my arms over my chest, tilting my head side to side.

"A few things. I don't believe that's any of your business though, is it?"

"Everything that happens in this town is our business."

Jax barked a laugh, causing Trent's face to turn red at the disrespect he felt he was too important to endure.

"You were a straight D student, your dad is the town's resident alcoholic, and you worked part time as a busboy at the diner before you started sucking the constable's dick. You don't have any authority here, princess." Jax's grin was smug. He had hit the mark, and he knew it.

The tension snapped like a rubber band. Saul lunged first, coming at me with all the finesse of a newborn calf. I sidestepped, grabbing his arm and wrenching it behind his back. He grunted in pain, and I shoved him forward, sending him sprawling on the street.

Mack swung at Jax, but Jax ducked, fluid and fast. He planted his knee into Mack's gut, doubling him over before grabbing his head in both hands and ramming his knee into Mack's nose. His scream was immediate, a steady stream of blood following quickly behind and pooling on the ground next to Jax's boots.

"Aww, come on. These are new."

He landed a clean right hook to Mack's jaw, shaking his hand out as Mack hit the ground with a thud.

Trent came at me with an uncoordinated punch, and I let it connect. His knuckles collided with my jaw, jolting my head to the side. For a moment, everyone went still. Blood filled my mouth, coppery and hot, and I spat it onto the ground at Trent's feet.

I laughed as I straightened up.

"My turn?" I asked him.

Trent's confidence wavered, his eyes darting to his friends. Jax was already on Mack again, kicking him square in the chest and sending him skidding across the cobblestones. Saul had barely managed to get to his feet before Jax turned on him, his expression cold and calculated.

Trent tried to throw another punch, but I caught his wrist, twisting hard until I heard the satisfying crack of bone.

"Tsk-tsk," I clicked my tongue at him, "I said it was my turn. Be polite."

I released his wrist, swinging out with my left hand at the same time and making contact with his temple.

He crumpled to the ground with a groan.

Mack and Saul had staggered to their feet, quickly scooping Trent up and throwing one of his arms over each of their shoulders and plodding away.

Jax came over to me, brushing the dirt from his jacket.

"Fucker got blood on my boots."

"Those were new." I frowned down at his now crimson-stained boots.

"I know!" he scoffed.

"Think he'll get them some better training after this?"

"Hopefully. Otherwise, where's the fun in it?" he replied, shooting me a grin.

We turned and kept walking, the implication of that interaction lingering in the back of my mind.

The constable was getting bolder, and he wasn't going to stop.

This was just the beginning, and we both knew it.

CHAPTER 30:

CAIRO

The front door slammed open, making me jump and nearly spill the steaming cup of tea I'd been cradling in my hands.

Radley strode in first with Jax right behind him, both of them looking like they'd just walked through a tornado.

Radley's lip was split, dried blood smudging his chin, but he seemed completely unfazed. His calm demeanor was mirrored by Jax, who's knuckles were red and raw, like he'd been boxing brick walls for fun.

"What the hell happened?" I asked, setting my mug down on the table and standing.

Radley flopped onto the couch with a sigh, his arm slung over the backrest. Jax walked over to the dining table, pulling out a chair and flipping it around before sitting, his typical smirk tugging at his lips.

"Ran into some old friends," Radley said, his tone light.

"Friends?" I shot him a look. "You look like you fought a bear."

Radley grinned, the split on his lip reopening slightly. "Close." He laughed, licking at the fresh blood on his mouth.

I narrowed my eyes at him.

"Three bears. Big ones." Jax snorted, leaning forward on the chair.

"It was nothing, Cai. The constable's usual lackeys. They didn't even put up a decent fight."

Radley turned his head to look at Jax.

"I don't know, they did a little better than last time."

"No, I think they're getting worse. Not a single one of those little fuckers can throw a solid punch. It's embarrassing."

"Indeed," Radley replied. He had tipped his head back to rest against the back of the couch, his eyes closed.

How was he so relaxed? Shouldn't there be like, adrenaline after a fight or something?

I think I could actually feel my blood pressure rising every time I was in a room with the two of them.

"So, the two of you frequently get into fist fights with the constable's gophers, then?"

Jax tilted his head from side to side.

"I wouldn't say frequently."

"I would." Radley laughed.

I pinched the bridge of my nose. How was the constable going to respond to that? If his grunts were an extension of him, and his power, I doubted he'd take it lightly if they continued to show up covered in their own blood.

"I can hear your wheels spinning from here, Cai," Radley mumbled from his spot on the couch.

"Is that not going to piss the constable off?"

"Possibly. He can get it too, if he wants it." Jax shrugged, pushing off the chair and walking to the fridge to collect two bottles of water.

He chucked one at Radley, hitting him square in the chest.

Radley let out a low grunt before slinging the nearest throw pillow at Jax's head and managing to connect all while still keeping his eyes closed.

"It was necessary, Torch. They were a warning. They may be a band of idiots, but they don't move without orders," Jax explained.

"Why is he so desperate to get to us?"

Radley straightened up, exchanging a glance with Jax as he twisted the cap off of his water and took a long sip before replying.

"If he is connected to the prophecy like we think he is and know that you are, you might be his target. We know he was working with my father, so he knows more about all of this than we do right now. Taking you out would make the prophecy useless."

Well, that was concerning.

"Sending his goons after us is just a flex, a reminder that he's watching," Jax mumbled.

The room went silent.

"So he's coming for me?"

"It's a possibility. We need to be ready, Cairo. Whatever he throws at us, we need to be able to handle it."

I swallowed hard, the gravity of their words hitting me like a ton of bricks. This wasn't just about survival anymore, this was about fighting back, about figuring out what the hell we were up against and facing it head on.

"We can handle it. I'll practice my Variances more," I said, trying to force an air of confidence into my voice.

Radley's smirk returned, confident and reassuring as he met my eyes.

"You are more powerful than me and Jax put together, we just have to fine-tune your abilities."

"No more yard fires," I said, nodding my head once in determination.

"Ideally," Radley agreed, pushing off the couch and sauntering over to me.

"Blood bother you?" he asked, wiping at his lip and checking to make sure his fingers came away clean.

"No."

"Good. You owe me a kiss."

He braced his hands on the back of the couch on either side of me, leaning in and pressing his lips gently to mine. Jax clapped quietly somewhere behind Radley, but I was focused on the way his tongue lightly traced my bottom lip, the faint taste of copper hitting me just before he pulled back, planting one more small peck against my cheek and then sinking into the couch next to me, his arm slung across my leg.

"About fucking time." Jax was grinning ear to ear, his legs kicked up on the coffee table as he raised his hand.

Radley rolled his eyes but raised his as well.

"Air high-five," he explained, a small smile warming his face.

CHAPTER 31:

CAIRO

"Push harder!" Radley yelled from the other side of the yard. He stood at what Jax had deemed a "safe" distance, coaching me through every possible route to access the rest of the magic inside me. It wasn't working. I could feel it, like a well of power laying within me, I just couldn't reach the damn thing.

Something was blocking it.

I squeezed my eyes shut and pushed as hard as I could against the wall that separated me from the magic, and still, nothing.

"It's not working." The words came out in a half-whine that made me cringe as I stretched my arms, feeling the tense muscles bunching beneath my skin. We'd been at this for hours. Radley had remained calm and confident, even as my frustration began bleeding into my voice every time I spoke. I, on the other hand, was growing increasingly irritable.

I was also hungry, so I'm sure that didn't help.

My patience had jumped out the window and fled to Mexico somewhere in the last hour, and if I didn't get a shower and a sandwich soon I was going to combust.

Possibly in a very literal sense.

"It will, we just have to figure out the right way to call on it," he said, his voice neutral.

He wasn't going to baby me through this, that was clear from the start.

"Easier said than done," I replied under my breath.

Jax had taken to shouting corny sayings at me with each failed attempt.

"When life gives you lemons, Cairo."

"You miss one hundred percent of the shots you don't take, Cairo."

"It's like taking candy from a baby, Cairo."

Sure. If the baby had a debilitating sweet tooth and a black belt in karate, then I'm sure taking candy from a baby felt just like this.

"What if Radley was in danger?" Jax mused, a mischievous grin splitting his face as he walked slowly toward him.

"Jax, whatever you're planning, don't."

He spun toward me, walking backwards as he spoke. "Planning? Me? I never plan."

Turning back around, he threw his arms out and launched Radley into the air.

"You motherfu—" Radley was cut off mid-sentence as he ascended near the tops of the trees.

"Better catch your man, Torch!"

"JAX!"

I ran as fast as I could, standing underneath where Radley was suspended in the air.

"He could break his neck from that height, you fucking goon!"

"Indeed. Better get him down quick, my arms are getting tired."

I raised my hands, calling on the only magic I'd managed to tame other than fire, and released shadows into the open yard around us. I willed them to wrap around Radley and drag him down, hoping and praying it would work.

Sweat beaded on my brow as I concentrated, focusing every bit of energy I had on getting him down safely.

"Come on, come on," I mumbled to myself, my arms beginning to shake under the force of the magic.

I heard Radley's muffled curses as Jax let him drop a few feet toward the ground, a cackle coming out of him as he did.

I turned my head to glare at him.

"So help me, Jax, I'm going to burn you alive."

"I'm comfortable with violence." He shrugged, completely unfazed by his dangling best friend and the threat of fire.

I growled in frustration at his unwavering smile and turned my focus back to Radley.

Closing my eyes, I began to envision the shadows as tendrils that stretched up above my head to wrap around Radley's arms and hook under his legs.

I tugged experimentally, letting out a relieved sigh as I felt his weight pressing against my magic, and pulled him slowly toward me.

"Cai."

I gasped, dropping my arms as my eyes flew wide open.

Radley was hovering in the air about three feet off the ground, until he wasn't. As soon as my arms lowered, he dropped the last few feet and hit the ground with a muffled grunt.

"Fuck! I'm sorry!"

He stood up, chuckling to himself as he brushed the dirt from his pants.

"The landing could use a little work, but you did good." His smile was blinding, a rare glimpse at his carefree side that always made his eyes shine just a little brighter.

I turned my head as the sound of someone screaming broke through my thoughts. Jax was running full speed around the yard, a handful of crows flying alongside him and taking turns swooping down and pecking at his head and neck as he batted his hands wildly around his face.

"I'm sorry! I'm sorry!" he yelled.

Radley huffed a laugh.

"Serves you right, jackass!" I yelled back.

Radley turned my face toward him with a finger under my chin.

"You can't be afraid of your magic, Cai. That's what is holding you back."

"I am afraid of it. I'm afraid I'm going to lose control, or that you're going to try to balance it and I'll end up hurting you."

"You have me, and you have Jax. We aren't going to let you combust. You have to trust us, and you have to trust yourself. This is *your* magic, Cairo. It wants to listen to you. Let it."

It made sense. You can't control something you're afraid of.

It didn't make the thought of hurting one of them any less terrifying though.

CHAPTER 32:

RADLEY

I managed to get Cairo out of the house after dinner. The monumental task of harnessing the power inside of her had been weighing heavy on her shoulders since we practiced in the yard. We spent a few hours in front of the TV afterward, her and Jax comparing their favorite scary movies while she lay sprawled out at the end of her couch with her feet resting on my lap. It felt so comfortable to have her there like that. And Jax, while he seemed easy going on the outside, had always been closed off when it came to new people. Not Cairo, though. He let his walls down around her as easily as he did with me, not an ounce of worry on his face as she got closer to the two of us. Somehow I knew she wouldn't take advantage of that, which only made the soft spot I had developed for her double in size.

The low rumble of the bike echoed through the quiet road, the sound as familiar and grounding as Cairo's heartbeat against my back. Her arms tightened around my waist as we leaned into a curve, her touch grounding me in a way I wasn't used to. The night air was crisp, carrying the sharp tang of pine and damp leaves from the woods lining the road.

The day had been exhausting. Digging through my dad's old journals, following cryptic leads, and feeling the noose of the prophecy tighten around all of us.

I hadn't told Cairo, but the way the townspeople were starting to look at her was unsettling. They were remembering her in fragmented pieces, a name whispered like a ghost in their minds. I wanted to believe they were harmless, but I couldn't shake the feeling in my gut that something was shifting, something we couldn't control.

We rolled to a stop outside the house, the engine cutting off with a cough. The sudden silence felt overwhelming, broken only by the hum of insects in the woods. Cairo slid off the bike and tugged at the hem of her jacket.

"You okay? I asked, watching her from the corner of my eye as I swung my leg over.

She nodded, brushing her hair out of her face.

"Yeah. Just tired, I guess. And a little…" She hesitated, her gaze drifting toward the dark tree line. "Does something feel…weird to you?"

I followed her line of sight, the woods darker than usual, as if the shadows themselves were thicker tonight. It wasn't the first time I'd felt it—a shift in the air, a tightness that clenched into the center of my chest like a warning.

"Yeah," I admitted, my voice low. "Something feels off."

Cairo turned to me, her brow furrowed over her stormy gray eyes.

"Do you think it's—"

A snap echoed from the woods, piercing the stillness outside. Both of us froze.

The silence that followed was too quiet, too calculated. My hand went instinctively to her shoulder, moving her behind me as I faced the tree line. Her knuckles brushed mine as if seeking reassurance as I used my free hand to reach for the knife tucked into my waistband.

Another crack, this time closer.

I opened my mouth to tell her to get inside when headlights flared down the road. A car engine roared, its tires spitting gravel as it skidded to a stop in front of us. Jax's car.

He threw the door open and half-jumped out, his expression wild.

"Get down!" he bellowed, his voice carrying over the sudden growl of something behind us.

I grabbed Cairo and pulled her to the ground as a shadow exploded from the trees.

The creature was massive, its shape twisting and writhing like smoke given form. Pale glowing eyes cut through the darkness, locking onto Cairo with a predatory hunger. Massive black claws that distended from something that vaguely resembled paws raked across the air, slicing through gnarled branches as it surged toward us.

"Stay down!" I yelled to Cairo, shoving her farther behind me as I moved to my feet.

Jax was already moving, a baseball bat in his hands. He swung it with precision, connecting with the creature's side. The shadow staggered, a guttural growl erupting from its misshapen form.

"Radley!" Jax shouted, tossing me a second bat.

"Got it!" I shouted back, keeping my eyes trained on the creature as it recovered, its form solidifying into something even more menacing as it honed in on Cairo. The shadow lunged toward her, and I sidestepped, swinging the bat in an arc. It caught the beast across its chest and it shrieked, the sound like nails on glass, but we didn't retreat.

Cairo scrambled to her feet, her hand outstretched. Her magic glimmered in the air like heat waves, a faint glow forming at her fingertips. The creature tracked the movement of her hands with its ghostly eyes.

"Cairo, don't!" I barked, the words sharper than I intended.

She hesitated, her power dimming.

"This thing doesn't want us," I said, my voice steady despite the adrenaline flooding my body. "It wants you. Stay back."

Jax flanked the creature, his bat swinging again, but it moved faster this time, ducking low and slashing out with claws that cut clean through the air where Jax had been standing. It caught the outside of his arm as he cocked the baseball bat back and brace to swing again.

"You good?" I yelled to him from across the yard. It was dark, but I could still make out the blood running from the claw marks on his forearm.

"Fine, keep her back!" He swung out again, missing the creature's front leg by an inch.

"Radley, I can help!" Cairo shouted, desperation dripping from her voice.

I gritted my teeth, pulling back and swinging the bat hard and striking the creature in the neck. It thrashed, its form flickering, but it wasn't enough.

"Then make it count," I growled, jerking my head toward her.

Her magic surged again, a semi-controlled burst that hit the beast square in the chest. The shadow exploded into tendrils of black smoke, the force sending all of us stumbling back.

For a moment, the woods were silent again, save for our ragged breaths.

"You okay?" Jax asked, his voice tight as he leaned on the dented bat.

"Yeah," I muttered, my eyes scanning the tree line for any signs of more creatures before moving to Cairo.

I reached out my hand and she stepped closer, placing hers in my open palm.

She trembled as I pulled her into my side.

"What was that?"

I shook my head, tossing the bat back to Jax.

"Something else to figure out. Add it to our list."

Jax snorted, his grin genuine despite the tension.

"Oh, good. I was just thinking that things were getting boring around here."

"C'mere." I reached my free hand toward Jax, he huffed but took a step toward me so that I could lay my hand over the cuts on his arm. Power flowed from my palm into his skin, knitting the flesh back together without so much as a bruise.

"Thank you, baby," he said, smacking a kiss on my cheek and quickly ducking my hand as he picked up the baseball bats and tossed them into the backseat of his car.

I rolled my eyes, but my attention had already shifted back to Cairo.

I leaned down to place a kiss on top of her head.

"You did good, Cai."

She was shaken but unharmed as her eyes met mine with a determination I hadn't seen before. Pride swelled in my chest, the scar on my wrist throbbing in response. She continued to surprise me. Each time her back was against the wall, she turned around and kicked right through it. The grasp she'd managed to get on her powers in such a short time was impressive for anyone, but for someone that hadn't grown up around here? It was astonishing. She was thrust into this world without even a basic understanding of what she was, and she was thriving. I tucked her in closer to my side, selfishly enjoying the way she fit against my body, and allowing the proximity to ease my racing heartbeat.

It seemed that we were safe for now, but one thing for certain, Cairo was stronger than she realized.

And we were going to need every ounce of strength for what was coming next.

CHAPTER 33:

CAIRO

The warmth of Radley's house wrapped around me as we stepped inside, though it did little to dispel the icy dread still stinging my chest. Jax slammed the door behind us, turning the lock with enough force to make the frame shudder.

"I'm going to have nightmares about that," I murmured, glancing back toward the woods. I half-expected another shadow to emerge, teeth bared and glowing eyes fixed on us.

"You and me both," Jax said, running a hand through his hair. His usual smirk was gone, replaced by a tightness around his eyes.

Radley's boots echoed on the hardwood as he strode to the window, pulling the curtain back just enough to peek outside. His broad shoulders tensed, his jaw ticking like he was still ready for a fight.

"What was that thing?" I'd never seen anything like it, not even in the scary movies I loved so much. It looked like it was made of smoke, so you would think you could pass right through it like fog, but it was solid. Teeth like razors filled my mind, raising the hair on the back of my neck.

"Honestly, I don't know. I've never seen one before. I saw something big moving through the woods toward the house, so I followed. I didn't expect that, though. Some kind of shadow creature? Someone sent it. We can guess who," Jax added.

Just another thing to add to our to-do list.

Figure out who sent the creepy fog monsters to kill me. Easy.

Had I been alone, I don't know that I would have survived it. Had Jax not shown up when he did, had he and Radley not been so in sync, I'm sure I would be dead. The whole thing was just a bit too close for comfort, making me feel more pressure than ever to gain control over my magic.

"You two work well together," I said, breaking the silence.

Radley snorted, letting the curtain fall back into place. "Yeah, well, it didn't start out that way."

I glanced between them, catching the flicker of a shared memory passing between them. Jax leaned against the wall, arms crossed, his expression unreadable.

"What do you mean?" I asked, curiosity bubbling up and overriding the palpable stress in the room.

Radley turned to me, a grin tugging at his lips despite the lingering seriousness in his eyes. "Jax here didn't always play for the good guys."

Jax groaned, dropping his head back against the wall. "Do we have to go there?"

"Oh, we're going there," Radley said, crossing his arms and leaning against the window frame. "She deserves to know."

Jax rolled his eyes but didn't argue.

"Back when I first met this idiot," Radley began, jerking a thumb at Jax, "he was working for the constable."

My eyes widened. "What?"

Jax sighed, his face darkening. "I was a kid, Cairo. The constable doesn't exactly give you much of a choice when he wants something."

Radley nodded, his expression softening just a fraction. "He recruits young—kids who are desperate, alone, easy to manipulate. Jax was one of them."

"I didn't know any better," Jax muttered, not meeting my eyes. "It wasn't like I wanted to work for him. But my home life wasn't exactly stable. He knew that, and used it to his advantage."

I stepped closer, my heart twisting at the sadness and regret in his voice. "What happened?"

Radley shot Jax a look, likely noticing the same tightness of his lips that I had, and cleared his throat before turning the conversation away from Jax's childhood.

"The constable sent him to Cheris's shop to, I don't know, intimidate her or something. I was there. Didn't like the look of him, so we had a little…chat."

"A chat?" Jax scoffed, finally looking up. "You punched me in the face."

Radley shrugged, unrepentant. "You were asking for it."
I covered my mouth to hide a laugh. "You fought him?"
"We had a scuffle," Radley said, his grin widening. "But I saw something in him—he wasn't like the rest of the constable's grunts. He had fight, sure, but there was something else. Something good."

Jax shifted uncomfortably under my gaze. "He offered to teach me how to fight properly after that. Said if I was going to throw punches, I might as well know how to do it right."

"And you quit working for the constable?" I asked.

Jax hesitated, his jaw tightening. "Not right away. It took some convincing. The constable doesn't let go of his people easily."

His eyes lowered to the floor. The furrow in his brow told me there was more to that story.

"But he got out," Radley said, his voice firm. "And now he's one of the good guys."

Jax rolled his eyes again, but there was a hint of a smile tugging at his lips.

I looked between them, a warmth spreading through my chest at their obvious love for one another.

"You two are something else." I laughed, shaking my head.

Radley reached out to ruffle Jax's hair, earning a swat in return. "Yeah, well, someone's gotta keep him out of trouble."

Jax grumbled something under his breath, but the corner of his mouth twitched upward.

As I watched them, I couldn't help but feel a strange sense of belonging—a thread tying us together, unbreakable despite everything trying to unravel it.

"Thanks for trusting me with this," I said quietly.

Radley met my eyes, his grin fading into something softer. "You're one of us, Cairo. We don't keep secrets from each other."

Jax cleared his throat, his usual smirk returning. "Unless it's embarrassing. Then all bets are off."

I laughed, the tension of the night easing just a bit as the three of us settled into the kind of quiet that felt like home.

CHAPTER 34:

RADLEY

The smell of garlic and onions sizzling in the pan filled the kitchen, blending with the low hum of the old overhead fan. Cairo leaned against the counter across from me, arms crossed, her face half-lit by the golden glow of the kitchen light. Her eyes followed the wooden spoon in my hand as I stirred the mixture into the pot of soup on the stove, the rhythm of it oddly calming given everything else going on in our lives.

"You're quiet tonight," I said, glancing up at her.

She shrugged, her lips curving into a small, tired smile. "Just...thinking."

I arched a brow. "Dangerous pastime."

That earned me a soft laugh, one that tugged at something deep in my chest. I didn't know how she managed to keep laughing with everything she was carrying, but damn if it didn't make me want to do everything I could to keep that sound around.

"Thinking about what?" I prompted, keeping my tone light as I turned back to the pot.

Her voice was quieter when she answered.

"How right this feels. Being in Hadeon, even with everything going on, it feels like where I'm supposed to be. Is that crazy?" I let her words settle for a moment, the only sound the bubbling of the soup. Then, on impulse, I dipped the spoon into the pot, blowing on it before turning to her. "Here, tell me if it's missing anything."

Her brows lifted in surprise as I stepped forward, leaning into her space and holding the spoon out to her. Her lips closed around it, and for a split second, my brain short-circuited, completely fixated on the way her mouth brushed against the wood.

Fuck me.

The sounds she had made in the shower flooded through my brain.

The image of her standing above me, her face flushed as she came apart on my mouth.

The blood in my body rushed south as I cleared my throat and attempted to gain control over my thoughts.

You are a grown man, not a teenage boy. Lose the fucking boner.

"Well?" I asked, my voice a little rougher than I intended.

She pulled back, the faintest pink brushing her cheeks as she swallowed. "It's good. Maybe a little more salt?"

I nodded, turning back to the stove to cover up how hard I had suddenly gotten. "Yes, chef."

There was a pause before she spoke again, her voice softening once more. "I never really cooked much before."

I looked over my shoulder at her. "No?"

She shook her head, her fingers tracing a loose thread on her sleeve.

"Life outside of Hadeon...it was just different. I never felt like I fit in, you know? Not in the city, not at school, not even at home, so I didn't really do much. I went to work, went to school, usually picked up takeout on my way home and ate it in front of my computer while I finished up whatever assignment I had."

"What about your step-dad?" She hadn't talked much about him, and I had never met him. She and her mother had lived alone most of time they had been in Hadeon, though they never seemed like they were missing a piece. I knew her biological dad had passed when we were young, but Alice never let Cairo feel his absence if she could help it. Alice was one of the best people I had ever known. Every time I had shown up to her doorstep covered in dirt and asking for a snack, she had led me straight to her kitchen and fed me while she cleaned my face. Between her and my mother, I never lacked a maternal presence.

I set the spoon down, turning to face her fully. She wasn't looking at me, her gaze focused somewhere distant.

"My dad—well, step-dad—he wasn't bad, just...distant. Everything was surface level. Small talk over dinner, the occasional pat on the shoulder. He provided, but that was about it. I don't think he ever really knew what to do with me. He fell in love with my mom, and I was just kind of an add on he hadn't really asked for."

149

"Sounds lonely," I said quietly.

Her eyes flicked up to meet mine, and there was something raw in them, something she wasn't used to sharing. "It was. And now that he's gone—he and my mom—I haven't even had time to process it. I'm just... here. And they're not. And I don't know how I'm supposed to feel about any of it, but the grief I thought would be here," she rubbed at her chest, just above her heart, "isn't really there, not in a consuming way. Instead I feel like I'm home for the first time in my life."

I stepped closer, slowly pushing her knees apart and settling my hips between them. The distance between us felt charged, every breath tight with the gravity of her words and the unspoken tension that seemed to follow us everywhere lately. Her gaze had dropped to where she was wringing her hands in her lap, so I gently lifted her chin with my forefinger, pulling her gaze back to mine before I spoke. She needed to know that she had a family, even if it wasn't the one she grew up with. We would never leave, we would never push her aside. We were here for as long as she'd have us.

"You're allowed to feel however you need to feel," I told her, my voice steady. "But you're not alone in it. You've got Jax and me now. You've got a family here. If this feels like home, it's because it is. You have always belonged here, Cairo. Right here."

She blinked, her lips parting like she wanted to say something but couldn't find the words.

"Always," I added, my voice dropping.

The look she gave me then almost made me forget how to breathe. Tears formed in the corners of her sweet doe eyes, the vulnerability in them nearly making me wince. I pushed her thick hair behind her ears, cupping the back of her head as I did and placed a soft kiss on her lips. She leaned into my touch, her mouth moving slowly against mine before she pulled back.

"Thanks, Radley," she said quietly, her voice thick with emotion.

I nodded, forcing myself to look away before I did something stupid, like sling her over my shoulder and carry her upstairs. "Always, Cai," I repeated, turning back to the stove. I gathered our bowls and ladled the soup into them, carrying them to the table as Cairo took her seat.

I watched her stir her soup absentmindedly, her spoon moving in slow circles. She wasn't really eating, just pushing the food around with her head resting on her hand.

"Do I need to add 'soup-eating lessons' to my list of teaching skills?" I asked, raising an eyebrow.

Cairo blinked, startled out of her thoughts. "What?"

"Soup," I answered, pointing at her bowl with my spoon. "You're supposed to eat it. Not hypnotize it."

She gave a small, reluctant smile, setting her spoon down with a sharp exhale. "Sorry. I was just thinking about the second prophecy."

I leaned forward, resting my elbows on the table. "What about it?"

Cairo let out a soft exhale, and I could almost see the wheels spinning in her head. "What kind of power do you think the constable has? I obviously got a boost from the one Nytheris created, so what did he get out of the second one?"

My playful grin faded as I studied her. "You're worried about facing him," I guessed, speaking softly. "That whatever he has is stronger, because it's darker."

She looked at me, her expression uncertain. "How can we make sure we win if we don't know what kind of power he holds? We just blindly follow the old 'good versus evil' cliche and hope we come out on top?"

"We don't have to know. Would it help? Probably. But we have something the constable doesn't: numbers. Yes, he has his little minions, but all of them have menial powers, nothing that would come close to touching yours, or mine and Jax's for that matter. You have us, that's our advantage."

Her lips twitched at that, but her gaze dropped to her soup again. "Quite the badass brigade we've assembled, hmm?"

I didn't hesitate. I reached across the table and laid my hand over hers. She stilled, but didn't pull away.

"You've got me," I said, voice firm. "You've got Jax. I've no doubt you also have my mother, Cheris, and anyone else in this town who is fed the fuck up with the constable and his band of dipshits. We will come out on top because we are better than him, in every single way."

For a moment, she didn't say anything. Then, her fingers curled under mine, holding my hand in a tight grip. "What more could I need?"

I grinned back at her, desperate to chase the worry from her face and smooth the lines that had formed between her brows. "Careful, or I'll start thinking you actually like me."

Her lips quirked up, and she picked up her spoon again. "Don't push your luck."

When the meal was finished, I collected our bowls and carried them to the sink, rinsing them out under the faucet. Behind me, I could feel Cairo's presence like a flame, warm and insistent.

"Radley?" she asked after a moment.

I turned, drying my hands on a towel. "Yeah?"

She stood a few feet away, her arms crossed. The expression on her face caused my pulse to quicken. Determination, resolve, a touch of anger, they were all there clear as day on that beautiful face. But her eyes? Her eyes held a hunger I hadn't seen since the bathroom the other day.

"I'm grateful for you," she said tenderly. "You know that? You've been like an anchor, ever since you busted into my motel room like a psychopath and borderline kidnapped me." She smiled, her tone playful as she took another step towards me.

"Well, lucky for you, I'm not going anywhere," I replied, my voice low as she prowled closer.

Her smile lit up her entire face, the light returning to her eyes and dancing around her irises.

I opened my arms as she took another step, closing my hands around her waist as soon as she was within reach and pulling her against me. Her gaze flicked to my mouth, her lips parted just slightly and for a moment, everything else faded—the town, the prophecies, the weight of our shared burdens.

"Radley…" she murmured, the breathy tone whittling away at any self-control I once thought I possessed.

And then her lips were on mine, rough and sure. Her hands found my shoulders, standing on her toes as I pulled her closer, my tongue chasing hers as the kiss deepened. The world narrowed to the feel of her in my hands. The way her mouth moved against mine, the smell of her hair as it brushed along my cheek. This was the shit they made movies about, the kind of kiss that made guys pick up guitars and wail into microphones. I dipped my hands lower, squeezing her ass in my hands and lifting her as her legs wrapped around my waist. Her breaths were coming in the sweetest little pants that had my jeans tightening painfully against my hardening dick.

How the fuck was I ever going to get enough of her—

The doorbell rang, the shrill noise shattering the momentum we were gaining.

Cairo pulled back, startled, and I groaned under my breath. "Of course," I muttered.

"Perfect timing."

We exchanged a glance, her cheeks perfectly flushed as she slid down my body and stepped away to straighten her shirt and hair.

I moved toward the door, pulling it open and having zero time to react before a body swept inside, hair smacking me in the face as the woman frantically made her entrance.

"Fucking pardon—*Mom?*"

"Cairo!" Mom's voice was trembling, her eyes bright with emotion. She spotted Cairo standing just outside the kitchen and rushed forward, crushing her in a tight hug.

Cairo froze in surprise, her eyes darting to mine as if to ask "what the fuck is happening" but Mom didn't let go.

"You're here," she whispered, her voice breaking. "You're really here. I remember everything."

I shut the door, my brows knitting together. "Mom?"

She pulled back just enough to cup Cairo's face, her hands shaking. "I remember Alice. I remember you, Cairo. Oh, sweetheart, I'm so sorry. I'm so sorry for forgetting."

Cairo blinked, looking overwhelmed. "Vesper…what are you talking about?"

"Goodness look at you. You grew up so good, Cairo. So beautiful, just like your mother. How have you been, honey? Where did you go? Oh, I have so many questions. I'm sure you do, too. We can talk about everything and—"

"Mom." My voice snapped her out of her frantic interrogation, her head bobbing in a nod before she got to the point.

Mom turned toward where I stood leaning against the door with my arms crossed, tears streaking her cheeks.

"Your mother," she said to Cairo, "she made a bargain to protect you. She gave up everything—her memories, her life here—so you could grow up safe."

Cairo's voice wavered. "I-I know about the bargain, but not the details."

Mom stepped back, her nose scrunching in disgust. "That man. Vance. 'The constable.'" She jerked her fingers in air quotes around the words as she spat them out. "I always hated him. The arrogance, the entitlement. I knew he was trouble"

Cairo's eyes bounced between my mother and me. "So it was him? He was the reason we left?"

I stepped closer, my stomach twisting.

"Why don't you sit down, Mom? We can talk about whatever you know."

Her gaze was solemn as she perched on the edge of the sofa. "I'm not sure why, honey. All I know is he was after the two of you like a dog with a bone. He harassed your mother for years, every time she ran into him in town he would follow her, threaten her. He was determined to get rid of the two of you but she never would tell me why."

Cairo's fingers brushed over the cracked leather, her expression a mix of wonder and dread. "I don't…I don't even know what to say."

I sat next to her, laying a hand on her leg, in an attempt to ground her.

"This is a good thing, Cai. We know more today than we did yesterday. It's a start," I said softly.

She looked up at me, her eyes shining with fear and gratitude, and nodded. Across from us, my mother was watching us with a gentle look, a smile tugging at the corners of her mouth.

I cleared my throat. "I'm going to make some tea, we need to go over every detail that you can remember."

Mom nodded, settling back farther on the couch as Cairo followed me to the kitchen.

"This could be good, maybe she knows something we can use against him."

"Well she knows more than we do, so that's already helpful." I smiled at her, checking to make sure that light hadn't been chased from her eyes again. Each revelation seemed to swallow a part of Cairo whole, overcoming her bit by bit until she shrunk into herself. I would take on the gods myself if that's what it took. A light like Cairo's was a rare thing, and watching it dim in the presence of the constable filled me with a righteous kind of rage that ate away at the back of my mind.

My wrist throbbed in response to the desperate desire to protect Cai, a subtle *thump thump thump* that fell in time with my heartbeat. Her hand came out to tenderly brush along my arm as she moved past me to pull the kettle out of the cabinet above the stove.

I would do anything to keep her safe.

It was more a fact than a thought, but terrifying all the same.

CHAPTER 35:

CAIRO

"My mother never mentioned why he wanted us gone?"

"He didn't want you gone, honey. He wanted you dead. But no, she refused to tell me why. The day you left, she came to me. She told me that she had made a deal, and that you two would be leaving and you wouldn't be able to return. I tried to pry the details out of her, but she wouldn't budge. 'Safer if you don't know,' is all she would say."

"Maybe it was the power? The thought of someone in town having more power than him must feel like sandpaper on that man's ego, so maybe that's all it was. I was a threat to his position, so he wanted me gone."

Radley shook his head. "It just feels too simple. How would he even know that you were the one from the prophecy?"

"The what?"

My head involuntarily snapped toward Radley, the 'oh shit' alarm blaring in my head as I replayed the words that had just left his mouth.

"What are you talking about? What prophecy?"

Radley sighed, moving to sit next to his mother and taking her hands in his.

"Mom, we have been looking into a lot of the things Dad was working on before he died, and a lot of them correlate with what Cairo is experiencing now. We found a hidden chamber in the archives, together Cairo and I managed to get the door open, and we found a prophecy inside. Apparently there are two, but that specific one...relates to Cairo."

"How? How can you be sure of that?"

Radley glanced at me before tugging the sleeve of his jacket up his arm, displaying his wrist to his mother as he spoke.

"Do you remember this? The scar?"

"Yes..." Her face scrunched in confusion as she traced the mark with her eyes.

"You got it when you were just a little bitty thing, I don't-I don't remember how."

"It was Cai. Mom, this mark, her ability to create it, it's a gift. There is no Variance that allows you to create a physical bond with another person, especially not at eight years old."

"So what are you saying?"

"I'm saying the prophecy talks about an ancient magic, the kind that can create a mark like this, the kind Cairo has displayed in front of me multiple times since she arrived."

"Well that could be—"

"We've seen Cheris. We've visited the ruins, and we have spoken directly with Nytheris herself."

Vesper's face paled, her hands coming up to muffle her gasp as she stared at Radley with wide eyes.

"No...that can't be right. I don't understand Radley, how could you possibly...You—"

"Breathe. We're okay. We're safe, we left completely unharmed. But she did confirm that Cairo is the daughter of the prophecy. There is no way around that, it's just a fact."

"Oh god," Vesper's voice was hardly more than a whisper, and all of the fear I'd felt since I arrived in Hadeon was mirrored in the soft breath of her words. Her eyes met mine, tears gathering in the corners of them as she shook her head slowly.

"My girl. I had no idea. If your mother knew, she never told me. I don't know how to help with this." She stood suddenly, coming to sit beside me on the couch and wrapping her arms around my shoulders. Her hand stroked through my hair as she rocked us back and forth in a soothing motion.

"Your mother, she did everything she could to protect you while she was on this earth. I will do the same now that she is gone. Anything you need, any way that I can help, you call me. No questions asked, do you hear me?" She placed her hands on my cheeks, her eyes darting between mine, waiting for me to agree.

"Yes ma'am, I understand."

She exhaled sharply through her nose, placing a light kiss on top of my head before moving to Radley and doing the same.

"I can't tell the two of you to leave this alone, I know that. But as a mother, I am going to tell you to be careful. You have resources in this town, people who want to see the constable put in his place. Use that to your advantage. Ask for help where you can, and lean on each other when you can't."

I swiped at the runaway tears under my eyes with the sleeve of my shirt, forcing a smile onto my face and nodding my understating to Vesper. She squeezed Radley's hand one more time and gathered her purse and coat.

"We will be careful, Mom. I promise. Whatever this is, she was chosen for a reason. And then she chose me. We will survive it."

Vesper nodded, her lips thinned in thought.

"Keep me updated, okay?"

"Of course."

We followed her to the door, closing it behind her and letting out a deep breath at the same moment.

"That was…a lot," Radley mumbled.

I exhaled, forcing my shoulders to relax. "Everything is a lot," I replied.

He lightly tugged on my elbow, pulling me into his arms and wrapping his own around my back. His chin rested on my head, and the way I felt wrapped up in him like this was so familiar.

"I meant what I told her, Cai. We will survive."

"We have no way of knowing that, Radley. I understand saying it to give your mom some peace of mind, but we still have no idea what we're up against with him. And I don't think we will until we're face-to-face."

"Then we keep training your magic, we make sure you are as ready as you can be, and then we go after him together. We figure out the second prophecy, we avoid whatever 'sacrifice' Nytheris thinks you will have to make, and we kick that fucker's ass. Happy endings only."

He nodded once. I could tell he was completely uncertain about his own words, but determined to make me believe them.

It was an adorable attempt, even if it wasn't successful.

"I just want to shut my brain off. I don't want to deal with any of this tonight." I raised my head to look at him, hoping he would hear the request I wasn't voicing aloud.

The way his hands tightened around me, I would say he got the message.

CHAPTER 36:

RADLEY

"Turn your brain off, huh?"

She nodded, her bottom lip rolling between her teeth as she looked up at me.

"I can help with that."

I lowered my hands, lifting beneath her thighs and pulling her into my arms.

The sweetest little squeak escaped her lips as her feet left the floor, coaxing a chuckle from my throat.

I squeezed my hands around her thighs, the feel of her beneath them making my jaw clench tight as I carried her up the stairs, entering my room and kicking the door shut behind us.

I slid my hands to her waist before lowering her to the bed and cupping her face in my hand.

"Lie back, and take your pants off for me."

She nodded quickly, scrambling to comply.

I took two steps back from the bed, watching her shimmy her pants off as I shrugged the jacket from my shoulders, then reached for the back of my shirt to pull it off. I tossed it to the floor before starting on my belt buckle.

"Panties too, Cairo. You aren't going to need those."

That gorgeous flush started at the base of her neck, traveling up and coloring her cheeks the most perfect shade of pink.

Watching her blush under my commands had my dick hard as a fucking rock.

I pulled my belt from the loops, unbuttoned my jeans and slid them down, watching the way her eyes tracked the bulge in my boxers with every move I made

I gripped it in my palm, stroking myself through the fabric slowly, reveling in the way her lips parted as she stared. She jerked her shirt off, reaching behind her and unclasping her bra and letting it fall from her chest.

Jesus fucking Christ.

"Tell me that you want this, Cai. Tell me that you're sure."

"Yes, I'm sure. I want you." Her voice was soft but determined.

"Lie back for me. Let me see you."

She obeyed, scooting back on the bed until her head met the pillows, and laying her legs flat against the bed, though they were pressed together tight at her knees.

That wouldn't do.

"Open your legs, Cai."

She bit her bottom lip again and hesitated, the pink tint to her cheeks flaming red at the request.

God she looked like an angel.

"You aren't shy are you?"

"Maybe a little?"

Well, we were going to have to fix that.

I prowled toward her, crawling up the bed until I hovered over her hips. I let one hand skate up her thigh, pressing my fingers into her hip as I moved upward, cupping her breast before continuing until my hand settled around her neck.

No pressure, just the presence of my hand against her throat to draw her attention fully to me.

"The only time you should be worried about keeping any of this hidden from me, is when I have pissed you off, which I plan to do as little as possible. Now, open. Your. Legs. Cairo."

I flexed my fingers against her neck, just enough to hear that sweet breathy moan, and felt her legs part beneath me.

"Good girl. Perfect." I used my grip on her neck to tilt her head toward me, taking her mouth the way I wanted to take the rest of her. My tongue slid along hers, the taste of her going straight to my dick, which I was currently grinding into her hip so hard I was worried I might hurt her with the friction of it.

I kissed down her jaw, moving my hand so I had access to her neck, and took my time licking and sucking a path down her chest, her stomach, stopping at her hips to leave a hickey at her panty line.

"Knees up, sweetheart," I rasped, rubbing her thighs as she moved them into position, giving me an unobstructed view of my favorite god-damn place on earth.

Her pussy was already glistening, and we'd been upstairs for less than five minutes.

My sweet, responsive, powerful fucking girl.

"Give me your hands?" She did as I asked, and I guided her hands to my hair, squeezing them into fists and encouraging her to use the same grip she had used in the shower.

"If this doesn't help, if you need me to stop, just tell me. Okay?"

"Okay."

Her grip tightened in my hair as I lowered my head, dragging my tongue in one smooth motion from her entrance to her clit, listening closely to the sounds she made so I could find the perfect rhythm to get her out of that beautiful head for a little while.

I wanted to take my time, I really did.

But her hips bucked upward, pushing her flush against my mouth, and I lost it.

I moved my hands underneath her, gripping her firmly in my hands and pulling her down on my tongue as I licked circles around her clit.

I opened my mouth wide, fitting her entire little pussy in my mouth, and sucked. She uttered a few curses before I stiffened my tongue and fucked her with it as deep as I could. Her pants grew rapid as my pace increased, but she needed more.

I moved one hand from underneath her, slipping two fingers in my mouth before sliding them inside her, curling them upward until I felt the little bundle of nerves that would set her off like a goddamn rocket.

"Radley!" Her back arched, one hand leaving my hair to grip her own as I moved my fingers faster.

"That right baby, just you and me."

"I'm gonna—" She pressed her palm over her mouth, stifling the sounds she couldn't hold inside.

I stilled my hand, raising my head. "Move your hand, Cairo. Let me hear you."

Her arm lowered slowly, soft whimpers falling from her lips.

"That's my girl. Scream my fucking name if want, but don't keep those sounds from me."

I moved my mouth back against her, alternating between licking and flicking my tongue around the most sensitive part of her, feeling her pussy flutter around my fingers as she hurtled toward the peak.

"Oh GOD."

She pulled hard on my hair, her hips grinding against my face as she came, squeezing my fingers in a death grip inside of her.

"There it is. So fucking perfect, Cairo." I pressed soft kisses to her inner thigh as she came down, slowly removing my fingers and crawling up the bed to settle my hips between her thighs. Her pupils were blown, her chest heaving and her hair disheveled from her pulling at it.

She looked wrecked.

She looked fucking perfect.

"Do you know how beautiful you look like this? All blissed out underneath me?"

Her smile was the cherry on top. The last brushstroke on a painting that would be displayed in the Louvre, or kept in a vault. I was attracted to her, obviously. But there was something deeper, too, something in my soul that ached for her. I wanted to pull my heart from my chest and knit it together with hers.

I was so fucked for her.

"More." Her needy whisper had me dropping my head to her shoulder, my lips finding that sweet spot between her neck and shoulder and sucking her skin into my mouth hard enough to leave a mark.

"I'll give you as much as you want."

She spread her legs open farther, arching her back so my cock rubbed against her, eliciting groans from both of us.

She raised her head, finding my lips with her own as I reached a hand between us and guided myself into her. Already slick from my mouth and her release, there was no resistance as I pushed in all the way to the base of my dick and started moving. Her nails dug into the skin on my back, the sharp sting spiking the pleasure coursing through my body and urging me to snap my hips faster against hers.

She rocked her hips into mine in response, her whimpers driving me forward at a punishing pace.

"Goddamn it, Cairo. You're going to kill me." My words were muffled, rasped into her ear, and her only answer was the way she pulled me tighter against her.

Each thrust grew sharper, the rhythm of my hips matching our ragged breathing.

The way her body molded perfectly to mine, the way she felt wrapped around me—every part of me—had something inside of me clicking into place. Something had broken deep in my chest the day I lost her, and now that she was back in my arms?

I had never been this whole in my entire existence.

I could feel my balls starting to tighten, the tingling at the base of my spine telling me what I already knew.

I was about to fucking come.

Hard.

I slipped a hand between us, using the other to prop my upper half up and keep my weight off of her while I stroked tight circles around her clit with my fingers, moving in tandem with her.

"One more. Come for me again, baby. Please."

I thrust harder, pounding into her at a relentless rhythm, the feel of her nails digging into my shoulders nearly enough to tip me over the edge.

"Oh fuck." Her voice was nothing more than a whine, needy and breathless as her thighs clenched around me, pulling me in deeper as her pussy squeezed my cock.

"Fuck." I pulled back, ready to pull out, but her thighs squeezed against mine, holding me in place.

"Birth…control." Her words came out as gasps, her eyes locking on mine.

"Are you on it?"

She nodded her head sharply. "Implant."

"Thank fuck." I crushed my mouth against hers, swallowing the greedy moans that fell from her lips each time I bottomed out. I buried my face in her neck, my fist clenched in the bed sheets as I pumped faster, coming inside her with a groan.

"Holy shit," she breathed. All I could do was chuckle in response. Holy shit, indeed.

CHAPTER 37:

CAIRO

Jax was in the kitchen by the time I got out of the shower, a bowl of soup balanced in his hands as he perched on the counter while Radley and I cleaned up the remnants of the dinner we had abandoned earlier. I submerged my hands in the warm soapy water filling the sink, pulled out a bowl, and scrubbed at it before rinsing it and handing it to Radley to dry. Our shoulders brushed as we worked, the close proximity sending chills down my arms after the way he had taken control of my body upstairs. His phone buzzed on the counter beside him, interrupting Jax's retelling of the first time he broke a bone.

He glanced at the screen and his expression darkened immediately.

"What's wrong?" I asked, drying my hands on the towel he'd been using.

"Cheris," he said, picking up the call. "What's going on?"

I watched as he paced the kitchen, tucking his free hand into his pocket as he listened.

"How many?" he asked sharply.

I exchanged a glance with Jax, who had been drinking his soup straight from the bowl, looking unbothered as usual. Now, his posture straightened as he slipped off the counter and set his bowl in the sink, his expression sharpening like a blade.

"We're on our way," Radley told her, ending the call. He grabbed his jacket, his movements quick and purposeful. "Grunts are outside Cheris's shop. She needs us."

I nodded, already pulling on my coat. Jax was beside us in an instant, rolling his shoulders as he shrugged his jacket on and fished his keys from the pocket.

We filed out the front door, Radley and me mounting the bike parked in the driveway as Jax walked toward his car.

"I'll follow you guys" He said as he climbed in the cab.

The ride into town didn't take long, but with each passing second I could feel my body beginning to tense, the cool night air against my skin doing little to calm my nerves as I sat behind Radley on his motorcycle. I had no idea what we were walking into, how aggressive they would be, if they had hurt Cheris. Radley was pissed, the creases between his brows before he flicked his visor down on his helmet giving away the anger that was building inside him.

Although his body was rigid in front of me, he reached back and squeezed my thigh reassuringly as we approached the square where Cheris's shop sat. Jax followed us closely in his car , pulling against the curb behind us as Radley shut the bike off.

Cheris was waiting by the door to her shop, displeasure distorting her features as she scanned the street in front of her. The moment she saw us, she ushered us inside, locking the door behind us.

"Thank you for coming," she said, brushing her hands against her apron.

"Where are they?" Radley asked. Cheris gestured toward the window, where the faint outlines of three men loitered in the shadows across the street.

"They've been there for over an hour now. Just watching. Waiting for something, perhaps."

"Why didn't you call sooner?" Jax asked, his voice sharp.

Cheris gave him a pointed look. "Because they haven't done anything yet. But they're here for a reason, and I wasn't about to wait until they decided to act. They just keep standing there, watching the door like they're waiting for someone to appear."

I stepped closer, lowering my voice. "Cheris, people are starting to remember me. Do you think that's what this is about?"

Her lips pressed into a thin line. "The mask is slipping," she answered softly. "And if people realize who you are...if he realizes, then I'm positive he would send his little shitheads before he faced you himself."

A chill ran down my spine, and I glanced at Radley, who met my gaze with a steady, reassuring look.

"We'll deal with it," he said firmly.

Before Cheris could respond, a distant scream tore through the square, a piercing, desperate noise that raised the hair on my neck in an instant. We all froze, the sound echoing off of the brick buildings.

Radley was the first to move, yanking open the door and stepping onto the sidewalk. I followed, my heart pounding rapidly in my chest. Across the square, something big was twisting its way through the darkness of the trees that lined the edge of the street, its shape shifting unnaturally as it darted between buildings. The shriek had come from a woman on the other side of the street who was now staring at the creature in abject horror.

"It's one of those shadow things," Jax muttered, his hand already on the hilt of a knife he kept tucked into his belt.

A second creature emerged to our left, its glowing eyes locking onto us as it ambled toward us on gnarled legs.

"Take the one on the left!" Radley shouted to Jax.

Jax didn't hesitate. He sprinted toward the first creature, his movements fluid and precise like he'd spent his life training to fight these monsters.

The second creature charged toward us, its claws scraping against the cobblestones as it picked up its pace. Radley stepped in front of me, his stance wide and his arms spread out far enough to block most of my body. A warm glow began building in his palms as his magic surfaced, ready to attack the thing coming toward us.

"I've got it," he said, his voice steady.

"Like hell you do," I shot back, summoning the familiar heat of my magic to my hands.

The creature lunged, and Radley moved faster than I expected, dodging its claws and landing a powerful punch to its side. A burst of light flared from his fists as he made impact, sending it skidding across the ground, but it recovered quickly, fixing its glowing eyes on him.

I raised my hands, aiming a blast of magic at the creature. The firelight erupted from my palms, piercing into its chest and forcing it back a few staggered steps.

Radley grinned at me over his shoulder. "Not bad."

"Focus, Radley!" I shouted as the creature regrouped and charged again.

This time, we worked in tandem. Radley darted in close, his fists glowing faintly with magic as he struck blow after blow. I kept my distance, sending bursts of fire to keep the creature off-balance.

Radley landed another blow in the center of the beast's chest, and with a deafening roar, it dissolved into smoke, its form dissipating into the night.

Radley turned to me, breathing hard, and offered a crooked smile. "Told you I had it."

I rolled my eyes, resting my hands on my knees to catch my breath as Jax came sprinting back toward us, blood dripping from a shallow cut on his arm.

"You good? Where's the other one?" Radley asked.

"Yes and dead," Jax said simply, wiping his blade on his pants.

The square was silent again, save for the distant sound of wind rustling through the trees.

"Think they'll send more?" I asked, my voice low.

Radley's jaw tightened. "Definitely."

CHAPTER 38:

CAIRO

A loud bell echoed through the square, the kind you'd find in an old church building, or apparently a small magical town in the middle of nowhere. Radley, Jax, and I exchanged wary glances as the people around us began filing toward the town hall, murmuring amongst themselves.

"What's that about?" I asked.

"Town hall meeting. Only one person rings that bell," Radley muttered, his jaw tightening.

"The constable," Jax added grimly, his hands shoved deep into his jacket pockets.

Radley nodded. "He's making a show of it. Wants everyone to know he's in charge."

We followed the growing crowd, the air thick with tension. The attack by the shadow creatures had shaken everyone, and now the constable was swooping in to take control of the narrative.

The town hall was packed by the time we got there, the wooden benches creaking under the weight of too many bodies. Radley led the way to a spot near the back, his hand intertwining with mine as we sat down.

The constable stood at the front of the room, his hands clasped behind his back. His outfit was immaculate, the polished buttons of his shirt gleaming under the dim lights.

Looks like someone missed out on all the fun out there. How convenient.

His eyes scanned the crowd, and for a moment, they locked onto mine. A flicker of something passed across his face—suspicion, calculation, maybe even recognition. When the room had quieted, he cleared his throat and began to speak.

"As many of you know, we've had an…incident in town," he announced, his voice smooth and commanding. "Two creatures—monsters—entered our square. Dangerous, unnatural things. Creatures made of shadows and some kind of dark magic."

Murmurs rippled through the crowd, people shifting anxiously in their seats.

"We were lucky," the constable continued, his tone grave. "Lucky that no one was seriously injured. But I fear this is only the beginning."

I could feel the threat in his words wash over the room like a wave of heat, stifling and oppressive.

"These creatures," he said, pausing for dramatic effect, "do not appear out of nowhere. They are drawn here by something—or someone."

My stomach flipped as his gaze swept over the crowd, lingering just a second too long on me.

"The only thing that has changed in Hadeon recently," he said, his voice dropping into a quieter, more ominous tone, "is her." He inclined his head toward me, the smallest hint of a smirk forming on his face. "Cairo Hallivand, isn't it?"

A ripple of unease ran through the room, heads turning toward me. My pulse quickened, and I forced myself to sit up straighter, meeting their stares head-on.

"Hallivand? Alice's daughter?" someone asked suddenly, their voice cutting through the murmurs.

The room went still.

It was an older man near the front gripping the back of the bench in front of him. He squinted at me, his expression both confused and resolute. "Where is Alice?"

I opened and closed my mouth enough times I probably looked like a fucking guppy. Clearing my throat, I let go of Radley's hand and stood.

"Yes, I am Alice's daughter. She isn't with me, she-she passed away, years ago."

How much did they need to know? "She had cancer. I came back to Hadeon on my own."

The silence was palpable, and the awkwardness of announcing my mother's death to a room full of strangers made me want to sit back down and bury my face in Radley's shoulder, but I wasn't going to back down from these people.

The older man stood up, looking to me before he spoke. "Constable, I don't know how she made her way through the barrier," he continued, his voice firm, "but Alice never would've raised a child who'd harm this town."

A chorus of agreement followed, voices rising in defense of my mother and, by extension, me.

"How could this possibly be her fault, anyway?"

"Alice's daughter wouldn't bring monsters here!"

"She belongs here as much as the rest of us."

The constable's expression froze, his eyes narrowing as he scanned the room. He hadn't expected this. He hadn't known that people were starting to remember.

His pale face darkened with frustration, but he forced a smile, raising his hands to quiet the crowd. "This isn't about assigning blame," he said smoothly, though his eyes darted back to me with barely concealed suspicion. "It's about keeping Hadeon safe. We need to remain vigilant. These creatures are a threat to us all, and we must be prepared for whatever comes next."

He let the silence hang for a moment before nodding curtly. "That's all for now. Stay close to your homes, and if you see anything unusual, report it immediately."

The crowd began to file out, conversations bubbling up as people discussed the creatures, the meeting, and, to my chagrin, me.

Radley touched my arm lightly. "You okay?"

I nodded, though my chest felt tight. "Yeah, I'm good."

Radley held up a finger to Vesper across the room, leaning in to place a quick kiss on my cheek.

"I'm going to walk her home, I won't be long. Stick with Jax and I'll meet you guys back here in a few minutes."

"Okay. Be careful." I waved to Vesper as they exited the building, weaving through the crowd until I lost sight of them.

I moved toward the doors in the sea of bodies, taking a deep breath of the cool air when I finally made it down the front steps. Jax wasn't far behind, his boots thudding along the ground as he caught up with me on the sidewalk.

"Well, it could have gone worse."

"You think so? He might as well have spray painted a target on my forehead."

"He should have, we could have used it for magic practice."

I swung my head toward him with a half-hearted glare.

"Hilarious."

"Cheer up, Torch. The only thing he accomplished was proving what we already knew. The people in this town loved your mom, and they aren't going to turn on you because Deputy Dickhead tells them to."

"You're right. I—"

I was interrupted by a hand clamping down on my elbow.

"Miss Cairo," the constable said, his voice low and smooth.

I spun around, jerking my arm out of his grasp and took a step closer to Jax, who had already moved closer to me.

"How about we all keep our hands to ourselves," Jax spit out, his fists clenched beside him as he spoke.

"Apologies, I was just trying to get her attention." The constable turned his gaze back to me, a saccharine smile plastered on his face that made my skin crawl.

"What can I help you with, Constable?" The words slid between my gritted teeth.

"I just wanted to clear the air, Cairo. Make sure there was no bad blood between us, so to speak." His smile grew, stretching across his cheeks in a way that made him look slightly deranged.

Probably is.

Jax spoke before I managed to form a semi-polite response. "We're all good. Thanks."

The constable hummed, his head cocking to the side as his eyes tracked mine.

"Well, I wasn't asking you, Jaxon."

I caught the wince on Jax's face from the corner of my eye. There was definitely a story behind that reaction.

A blonde head bobbed closer to us through the remaining stragglers, her pace clipped as she weaved her way over to us and planted herself at an alarmingly inappropriate closeness to the constable.

"Hello Jax, Cairo." Her voice dripped with fake sweetness as she spoke.

"Ava," I replied, giving her a small nod.

"It's Anna."

"Sure." I bobbed my head in a lazy nod, which only served to piss her off further. I held back an involuntary smirk.

Her head tilted to the side as she spoke, "Did you let Radley off the leash already?"

Is it possible to actually roll your eyes into the back of your head? I think I just saw my spine.

"Yes, Amanda, he's been a very good boy lately, so I gave him a little lee-way."

The glare she shot me could have melted steel.

"You're just hilarious, aren't you?"

"It's a blessing and a curse."

"Jax?"

The pretty waitress from the diner stopped next to him, apron in hand.

"What's going on over here?" she asked, her voice light, but she was taking in the situation with sharp eyes, her hands clutching and relaxing over and over again on the bulk of her apron.

Her eyes darted to mine, giving me a nearly imperceptible nod before turning back to Jax.

"Lenny." Was Jax…blushing? Oh god, that's cute. I watched the two of them exchange awkward small talk, nearly forgetting about the constable and his blonde sidekick until he grabbed my arm again.

He leaned in, voice low enough that only I could hear him as he spoke directly into my ear. "I don't know what game you're playing, but I'm watching you."

"I'm not playing any games," I responded, keeping my voice steady despite the fear curling in my stomach.

His smile was thin and sharp, like the edge of a knife. "We'll see about that. You would do well to keep out of my way, honey. I'd hate to have to show you why I am both respected and feared in this town."

He released my arm and strode away, his boots clicking against the cobblestones and Anna following on his heels.

Radley appeared back at my side when I turned around, his breathing labored like he'd run all the way back to the square. "What did he say to you?"

"Nothing I didn't already know," I muttered, though my voice was shakier than I intended.

Radley's eyes narrowed, his jaw tight with barely restrained anger. "He's got a target on you now."

"He's always had a target on me," I said quietly.

Jax excused himself from Lenny and joined us, his expression unreadable.

"Well, there's at least one more person in town who sees through his bullshit." He bumped my shoulder. "She's a Temper, not that it had any effect on him since the only magic he was using was his super ability to be a major fuck rag, but she tried to help." He shrugged, the shyness he was displaying so at odds with the extroverted Jax I had come to know.

"A Temper?" I needed a magic for dummies book at this point.

"It means she can temper the abilities of those around her. Not a super strong ability, but it's a decent one to have when things get out of control," Radley answered, his gaze moving around us like the constable would come running back any second.

I nodded. "Tell her thank you for me."

Radley reached for my hand, wrapping it in his and finally pulling his focus back to our group.

"So what's the plan?"

I looked between them, my resolve hardening. "We keep going. We find out everything he doesn't want us to know. And we stop him before he stops us."

CHAPTER 39:

RADLEY

A dense fog had rolled in the night before, covering most of the back-yard. Jax and I worked side by side in the early morning sun, setting up targets and hanging empty bottles from the lower tree branches. Our only priority right now was getting Cairo to unlock the full potential of her magic. Her Variance appeared to be Flame, and judging by the blasts she had aimed at the creatures last night, she had a pretty good grip on that. But then there was the other thing. The void she had managed to produce around us the first time we trained was shocking.

Not only was that not a known Variance, but to create something of that magnitude on the first try? It was unheard of. Whatever else was laying inside her, waiting to be honed and wielded, it was strong. The fire from her hands never affected me, but the void had caused a deep throbbing to start in the mark on my wrist, a clear sign that it was a gift from Nytheris and not a part of her Variance.

We just needed to get her out here and push her until she broke through whatever wall was holding her back from accessing all of the power that was brewing beneath her skin.

She was strong, I already knew that. But what would she be like when she was fully untethered?

"So what is the game plan here?" Jax asked, arranging the last wooden target next to me.

"We focus on her fire first, get her to hit as many of these," I gestured to the dozens of bottles dangling from the trees around us, "as possible, and then once her blood is pumping and she's loosened up, we push."

"Push," he parroted, his voice dull.

"Yes. There is more underneath there than the Void, we just have to call it out. She doesn't know how yet, so we are going to have to help her."

Jax let out a low whistle, running his hands over his short hair.

"If she gets pissed, I'm leaving and letting her kick your ass."

"She won't. She wants this as much as we want it for her. We all know how important it is that we're as ready as possible."

He nodded, pulling out his phone with a smug grin as he typed out a text.

"Now who could you be talking to with that look on your face?"

"What? There's no look on my face. I'm always this handsome."

"Wouldn't happen to be a certain redheaded waitress, now would it?"

His head whipped up, eyes wide as he gaped at me.

"How the fuck would you know that?"

"Jax, she asks about you every time she sees me. She's been into you for years, buddy."

"You didn't want to clue me in on that, jackass?"

I shrugged. "In my defense, I did tell you. The first three times she asked about you. I figured you weren't interested."

"Fair enough. Just too much going on, you know? Never really had time to think about getting attached to anyone."

"Except me."

He slung his arm around my neck in a headlock and rubbed his fist over my hair while he cooed, "Except you, Raddy-kins."

I shoved him away from me, smoothing down the locks he'd knotted together.

"And your girl, of course. She's pretty alright too."

"Yeah, she really is."

"How's that going, by the way?"

"The girl I've loved since I was a kid randomly showing up back in town fourteen years after I last saw her, the prophecy that demands she sacrifice herself to save all of our lives, or the souvenir that neither of us knows anything about?" I held my wrist up to him as I spoke, gesturing to the one undeniable link I had to the past Cairo and I shared.

"All of it. We haven't talked much about how you're dealing with all this, man. It's a lot."

I considered the magnitude of his question. Before Cairo came back to town, Jax and I spent most of our time fucking around with my bike in the garage, or chasing the goons away from the little businesses on the square.

There wasn't much stress, but there also wasn't much going on. Cairo came in like a hurricane and flipped everything upside down, but somehow the world made more sense on its head. She breathed life into everything around her. Her laugh, her smile, the way she just fit perfectly with us.

"I'm good. So much shit has changed in the last two weeks, but I don't regret any of it. Having her back, seeing her every day, it's like a gift, man. I could do without the looming threat of danger, but I wouldn't trade it if it meant losing her again."

"I've seen the googly eyes when you look at her, you're in deep there." His eyes searched my face, looking for a reaction.

"Is that a bad thing?"

"Not even close. She's a good girl, Radley. She carved out a soft spot for herself in both of us, I just don't have the urge to smush my face against hers like some people."

"You're missing out. I'd have to kill you if you tried, though."

He held his hands up in front of him.

"No worries, buddy. She's always safe with me though, you know. If you aren't around, I've got her."

"I know." I nodded. And I did. I knew that if it came down to Jax or Cairo, he'd throw himself in front of a train before he let her get hurt. In such a short amount of time, she drew us both to her like magnets. We were completely sucked into her orbit.

And there was nowhere else I'd rather be.

She was like a missing puzzle piece. Her arrival had shifted everything back to where it was supposed to be, and there was indisputable rightness in how she fit in here. I'd thought about her so much over the years when she was gone. The first few years were the worst. I was just a kid who had lost his best friend in the middle of the night and no one around me had any answers. The older I got, the more I learned, and the angrier I became. What if I could have fixed it? Kept them safe? That of course, was the angsty ramblings of a teenage boy who experienced his first heartbreak in a relationship that didn't even exist. Cairo had taken a piece of my heart with her when she went, and she was collecting more and more of it every day that she was here next to me. By the time she came back to

Hadeon, I was terrified. I knew there was a threat, but I had no idea who or what it was. The idea of losing her fully made my chest ache, which was exactly why I'd tried to get her to leave that first day.

At least now we knew what we were up against. Cairo was growing stronger every day, and we were getting closer to the answers we needed.

When this was all over, when she was safe, I would gladly hand over the rest of my heart. I think it had always belonged to her, anyway.

CHAPTER 40:

CAIRO

The sound of three glass bottles shattering had my adrenaline pump-ing. Over the last hour, I had learned how to direct my magic to hit different objects in unison. One blast leaving my palm and splitting into three separate streams of fire that hit the targets dead-on.

Jax and Radley looked at me, their mouths agape.

"No one is going to clap? That was fucking good!"

"We aren't clapping because we're in shock, Torch. What the hell was that?"

"What do you mean?"

"How did you split the fire?"

"I don't know, I just like, told it to?"

Jax turned to look at Radley, rubbing his hand over his jaw in bewil-derment.

Radley pushed off the tree he'd been leaning against and walked toward me.

"You 'told' it to split?"

"Yeah, I mean, I just pushed it outward and then imagined it separat-ing. I actually was going for four streams, but I still feel like three is pretty good, right?"

"It's incredible, Cai. We just haven't seen anything like it. Ever."

Jax nodded in agreement, still looking stunned. "I've met plenty of Flames, and none of them were able to split the blast like that, at least not that I'm aware of."

I frowned, looking down at my hands. I could feel the magic in them, a steady flow that started somewhere in my chest and ran through my veins. It was like lightning beneath my skin, but it responded to my commands; it answered to me. That was a good thing, wasn't it?

"I think we're ready to see what else you've got." Radley stood in front of me, his arms crossed and his face relaxed, but I could see the tension in his posture. Whatever magic was stuck inside me, he was worried about it.

"I'm ready."

Jax kicked aside the remnants of the scorched targets littering the ground at our feet and then took a few steps back.

"You've got something big in there, Cairo. Let it out."

I nodded, shaking out my limbs and adjusting my stance for the wave of power I would hopefully be able to summon.

"Close your eyes," Radley instructed, keeping close to my side. "Forget about the targets, forget about everything going on. Find where that power is locked up and reach for it."

I did as he asked, the world around me fading out as my eyes fluttered shut. The distant sounds of the woods around Radley's house faded into the background as I traced the lines of power through my veins and back into my chest where they began.

My magic simmered there, familiar and warm, but it wasn't what I was looking for. I needed to go deeper.

I inhaled slowly, urging my muscles to stay relaxed as I delved beneath the bright ribbons of my power, forcing myself further down until I hit a wall.

It pulsed under my touch, my breath quickening as I coaxed it to open.

"Don't stop," Radley said, his voice cutting through the haze of my mind. "You've got it, Cai."

I braced myself, focusing all of my strength on pushing through the wall in front of me. Sweat beaded on my forehead, my muscles trembling with exertion as I strained against it and the air around me thickening and pushing down on my chest.

Don't stop, Cairo.

Almost there.

Just a little more…

The barrier snapped, flying open like a dam giving way, and a flood of power surged through my body.

Light burst from my skin, the flash so bright I could see it from behind my closed eyes. A gasp escaped me as the magic flew through every vein, every cell in my body.

It was overwhelming, it was terrifying, it was—

Euphoric.

I heard Jax let out a low whistle. "Holy shit."

"Cairo…" Radley's voice was soft, reverent, like he was seeing something extraordinary.

I opened my eyes, marveling at the way my skin was glowing. Like a thousand tiny lights shining through my flesh. It was breathtaking.

The light moved, flickering and dancing across my arms like flames. The entire backyard was illuminated, like a spotlight had been placed over it.

And then, something changed.

The power inside me grew hotter, sharper, burning like it was trying to claw its way out of me. It felt like that first day in the archives, only worse.

My breath hitched as the light flared brighter until it was almost blinding. My muscles locked, agony tearing through me under the weight of trying to hold it back.

The euphoria vanished, replaced by an unbearable pain that ripped through my entire body.

My eyes felt like they were melting in their sockets, tears streaming from them with each blink.

"Radley!" I screamed, my voice cracking over his name. My knees gave out, buckling as I hit the ground and clutched at my torso like I could physically hold the magic inside of me.

"Cairo?" His voice was full of panic, his knees hitting the ground beside mine. I squeezed my eyes shut, tears spilling down my cheeks as the magic roared inside of me, threatening to consume me whole.

I was going to die.

I was going to burn alive.

I reached my hand out blindly to shove Radley away from me.

If I was going to explode, I refused to take him out with me.

He caught my hand in his, his grip firm as he intertwined his fingers with my own. The second our skin touched, the pain eased.

The burning receded, the light dimmed, and the crushing weight in my chest lifted, like a storm passing through.

I clutched his hand tightly in mine, gasping for cool air to soothe my burning lungs. The light was slowly fading from my skin, the tremble in my muscles easing just a fraction.

"Cai." Radley's voice was filled with awe, drawing my attention to our joined hands that he was staring at with wonder scrawled across his face.

Then I saw it.

The same golden light that had nearly ripped me apart, now coursed gently through him.

A faint glow shimmering along his skin, all the way up to his neck.

His jaw clenched, eyes widening in shock as he looked at me.

"I can feel it, I can feel your magic under my skin."

I stared back, too stunned to form a reply.

"Are you okay?" he asked softly.

I nodded weakly, though my body felt like it had been put through a taffy stretcher.

"What happened?"

Radley glanced at our joined hands, then to Jax who was crouched a few feet in front of us, his hands on his head and his face a mask of worry.

"Do you remember what Nytheris called me?"

I sifted through the melted remains of my brain, trying to remember everything she had said to us that day at the ruins.

"She called you the one who 'tethers' me."

Radley nodded.

"A tether for your power. It's too much on your own, it will overwhelm you. But this," he ran a finger over the mark on his wrist, "this lets me share the burden with you, if it flows through both of us, it's manageable."

I let his words sink in. Of course it made sense.

Did it only work because Radley was a conduit? Would it have worked if I had bound myself to someone else as a child?

I would give anything to go back to that day.

How did I even know to do that? Why would I?

Every revelation opened the door to more questions.

Whatever I had just unlocked now roamed freely under my skin, waiting for me to call on it again.

I just hoped Radley would be there if I ever needed to use it.

CHAPTER 41:

RADLEY

I spent the rest of the day laid up in bed with Cairo, most of the time just watching her breathe while she slept, savoring each deep inhale she took after the toll the day had taken on her mind and body.

We finally left the bedroom around six, opting to sink into the large couch in the living room with some tea. Her head was in my lap, some old show she was obsessed with playing quietly on the TV in front of us.

I ran my fingers over her dark hair, smiling at the sweet sounds she made with each pass.

"How are you feeling?" I asked. Her color had returned a few hours ago, but there was no chance she wasn't sore as hell after what she had gone through.

"I'm okay. A little achy, but sleeping most of the day seems to have helped."

I nodded. "Makes sense. Sleep helps kind of recharge when you overdo it with magic. We were always told to rest after practice when we were younger."

"Do you think—" She was interrupted by the sound of the front door slamming open, causing us both to sit up straight as Jax barreled in.

"Radley!" he yelled, stopping just beside the couch. "I've been calling you. There's something going on in town. I'm headed that way now."

"Fuck, I left my phone in the kitchen earlier." I jogged over to the counter, picking it up and glancing at the screen. Ten missed calls. All from Cheris, Jax, and my mom.

"Shit," I muttered, swiping to unlock it just as it buzzed again. "Mom" flashed on the screen. Without hesitation, I answered.

"Mom?"

Her voice came through, frantic and sharp. "Radley! The town, it's overrun. There are these-these creatures everywhere."

My stomach dropped. "What? Where are you?"

"I'm at the diner, helping people barricade themselves inside. But they're everywhere, Radley. I don't know how much longer we can hold them off."

I exchanged a look with Jax, who had already grabbed his car keys. Cairo stepped closer, her face set with determination.

"We're on our way," I told her, hanging up and shoving the phone into my pocket.

Cairo's voice was calm but firm. "Let's go."

"You okay to do this?" I asked her.

"I'm fine." She nodded, the look on her face not leaving me any room to argue, despite how badly I wanted to lock her upstairs until all of this was over.

But we didn't have time to debate. Turning on my heel, I followed Jax to the driveway.

We sped toward town in Jax's car, the engine roaring as it tore down the cobblestone streets. Cairo sat in the backseat, gripping the edge of the seat with white-knuckled hands. Her magic buzzed faintly in the air around her, like it was waiting to be unleashed.

The moment we hit the edge of town, chaos unfolded in front of us. Shadow creatures darted between buildings, their dark forms contorting monstrously in the light of the streetlamps.

People screamed as they ran for cover, slamming doors shut as they barricaded themselves inside.

I threw the door open before Jax even fully stopped the car. "You take the left side!" I yelled to Jax. "Cairo, stay with me!"

She leaped out behind me, nodding as she summoned a flicker of light into her palm. The first creature lunged from an alley, its spindly claws scraping along the cobblestones. I darted forward, pulling magic through me and channeling it into a kick that sent it sprawling. Cairo followed up, her magic surging out in a sharp burst that struck its shadowy form and sent it dissipating into the air.

"Radley!" a familiar voice called. I turned to see my mother standing near Cheris's shop with a group of townsfolk. She clutched an iron poker in her hands, her eyes fierce.

"Mom!" I shouted, running toward her. "You shouldn't be out here!"

"Neither should you," she snapped, swinging the poker to knock back a creature that got too close. "But here we are!"

Another shadow creature lunged, and Cairo's magic flared bright, hitting it mid-leap. It shrieked and dissolved, the sound cutting through the night like nails on a chalkboard.

Jax came sprinting around the corner, his knuckles bloodied. "East side's bad—there are too many of them," he huffed out, breathing hard.

Cairo wiped sweat from her forehead, her expression grim. "We can't hold them off like this forever."

"We don't have to," Mom said, her voice cutting through the chaos. She jabbed the poker at the sky. "We just need to drive them back long enough for the town to regroup. They're drawn to magic, so stay focused on protecting each other!"

Her words were punctuated by another scream, this time from the direction of the main square.

"I've got it," Jax called, already moving.

"Wait—"

He didn't stop. I growled in frustration but turned my attention back to the street as three more creatures emerged from the shadows.

"Cairo?" I asked, holding out my hand in offering.

She nodded, her chest heaving. "We can do this."

"Focus on me. I've got you."

We stood side by side, her magic crackling like lightning in my veins as it flowed from her palm into mine. The creatures were fast, but they weren't smart. Every time one lunged, we worked in tandem to take it down. A pair of them approached us, their limbs cracking with each step as they prowled forward. Cairo raised her free hand, aiming toward the one on the left, and I mirrored her movements, focusing my attention on the one to the right. Light and fire erupted from our outstretched palms in controlled streams, obliterating the beasts on impact, leaving nothing more than ashes behind.

Another creature barreled toward my mother, and I moved on instinct. I turned, pulling Cairo with me, and slammed my magic into the earth beneath my feet, sending a surge of energy that tripped the creature up long enough for mom to swing her poker and knock it back.

"Thank you, honey," she said, her voice tight.

"There are more," I replied, scanning the area for the others that I knew were there.

I saw the questions in her eyes as she watched Cairo and I work together. The magnitude of the power we were wielding was impossible to hide, and I knew I was going to have to explain it sooner or later.

Just not now.

Cairo let out a sharp gasp, and I turned to see her staring toward the alley beside Cheris's shop. A single creature stood there, larger than the others. It seemed to watch her, its head tilting unnaturally as if it recognized her. Then it turned and bolted, moving toward the shop.

"Cairo, wait!" I called as she released my hand and started after it.

"I can't let it get to Cheris!" she yelled over her shoulder, already sprinting down the alley.

"Dammit," I muttered, hesitating. "Be careful!"

Mom grabbed my arm. "Let her go," she said. "She won't go far, and we need to help as much as we can."

I clenched my jaw but nodded, turning back to the street. The town wasn't safe yet, and there was no time to argue.

"Stay alive, Cairo," I whispered, sending a silent wish after her as she disappeared into the darkness.

CHAPTER 42:

CAIRO

I was still catching my breath when the creature's last remnants faded into the night air, leaving only the faint scent of ash and decay behind. The atmosphere around me buzzed with the energy of the magic I'd just used, but for a moment, I let myself feel the victory, the relief. We had stopped one more of the monsters from terrorizing the town.

But that relief didn't last long.

I stepped back from the alley, wiping my brow, and turned toward the main road. I had a sizeable cut traveling the length of my forearm, but other than that I was in one piece. My thoughts were already racing ahead to Cheris's shop. I needed to make sure she was okay, grab a rag for my arm, and find Radley.

The feeling of being watched crept over me, suddenly putting me on high alert.

I froze. Across the street, I saw him. A man stood by the lamppost, his back slightly turned, talking into a phone. But something about the way he was standing—like he was waiting—made my blood run cold.

I took a few cautious steps toward the corner of the street, hoping to stay out of his line of sight. But the second I moved, I saw him glance in my direction. His eyes met mine briefly before he turned away and spoke quietly into the phone again.

My heart hammered in my chest as I turned on my heel and sprinted toward Cheris's shop, my arm pressed tightly against my chest to staunch the bleeding.

I couldn't afford to wait. The man hadn't moved and he was still on the phone, but his presence loomed over me, a constant threat. Every instinct in my body screamed to keep moving, to get inside, to make sure Cheris was safe.

I reached the door and shoved it open with force, slamming it behind me as soon as I was through. My breath came in ragged gasps, my pulse racing from the run.

"Cheris!" I called, panic in my voice.

She didn't answer right away, but I heard her footfalls on the floorboards as she appeared from behind the counter. Her eyes scanned me quickly, locking onto my arm where a long gash had opened up from the earlier fight. Blood was trickling down my wrist, but I hardly noticed it in the chaos of the moment.

"Cheris, there's a man outside," I said quickly, my eyes darting toward the window. I could see him through the crack in the blinds, still standing in the same spot. A blonde head appeared from the curtain behind the counter, moving into the room at a lazy pace with her usual smug smile firmly in place.

"Hello, Cairo."

Cheris didn't flinch, just calmly moved toward the door, checking the locks. She turned the deadbolt with a soft click.

"Sit, child." Her voice was steady, almost comforting, as she gestured toward one of the chairs near the counter.

I hesitated for a moment, watching as Anna moved to a stool and sat down, not saying a word. The exhaustion of the night mixed with the blood loss was starting to hit me, and I reluctantly obeyed, taking a seat.

"I need to get back out there, Radley and Vesper are still outside."

Cheris moved around the room with a practiced grace, grabbing the supplies she needed to tend to my hand. Her movements were slow and deliberate, her face calm but her eyes sharp, as if she was aware of something far beyond what was happening in the moment.

"You're hurt," she murmured as she knelt beside me, peeling back the fabric of my sleeve. "Let me patch this up and then you can go, I'll be quick."

I glanced out the window again, seeing the darting shadows of creatures fighting in the streets. The town was in chaos. The beasts were dwindling, but the fight was far from over. I knew Radley, Jax, and the others were out there, holding their ground.

"I'll be fine," I said, trying to push past the dizziness that was creeping up behind my eyes. "It's not bad. Why is she here?" I asked, nodding toward the bitch at the counter.

Cheris met my gaze, her expression softening. "Ignore her. Tea will help," she insisted, moving toward the stove. I couldn't argue with that; the warmth of tea always had a way of calming me.

She placed a small, delicate cup of the steaming liquid in front of me, her eyes glinting with something unreadable. The fragrance of the tea filled the room, earthy and sweet. Without thinking, I picked it up, savoring the warmth against my hands as I took a small sip.

The dizziness worsened with every passing moment, but I tried to stay focused. My mind was a whirl of questions, of concerns. The relentless feeling of unease that we'd faced in just the last few hours—the creatures, the strange man, the looming sense that something was coming for us— was too much. I needed a moment, just a moment to breathe.

Cheris sat next to me, taking the bandages from her kit and wrapping them carefully around my hand, her touch gentle and precise.

"You know my Variance," she began quietly, not looking at me, but her voice carried weight. "I am blessed to see things, but I cannot always speak of them. It's a double-edged sword, Cairo."

I blinked, trying to clear the fog in my mind. My head felt heavy, the world around me slowly beginning to tilt.

"I need you to understand what I'm about to tell you, Cairo," she continued, her voice growing softer, more urgent. "You will survive what comes next. It will make you stronger. It will make your bond with him stronger."

I furrowed my brow, confused and alarmed by the cryptic words. "What things?" I managed to whisper, my dizziness increasing to the point where I could no longer hold onto the cup.

Why the fuck am I slurring? I didn't lose that much blood.

I set it down on the counter with a soft clink.

Cheris paused for a long moment, her eyes steady and filled with sorrow. "I apologize for my role, though it is a necessary one," she said, her voice thick with emotion. "Stay strong, child. You were made for this."

I couldn't hold my head up anymore. My vision swam, the edges of the room blurring. The dizziness was too much. The tea, or something else, had clouded my senses, and I struggled to stay awake. My head fell forward, but was saved from cracking against the table by Cheris's hand, which she used to cup my cheek and lower me gently to the cool wood of the table.

I heard the door creak open slowly, the sound too distant to be real at first. My head snapped up in time to see Cheris's eyes narrow, and the low murmur of a man's voice followed.

The constable.

"Your time will come," Cheris stated coldly, her eyes sharp as she faced him, unafraid.

"You'll get what you deserve, Constable."

"Anna, help me get her to the car." His voice was harsh.

I couldn't hold my eyes open any longer. My world went black as the voices faded into nothing, the last words Cheris spoke to me echoing in the distance.

Stay strong, child. You were made for this.

CHAPTER 43:

RADLEY

The minutes dragged by as I fought to keep the creatures at bay. The entire town was on edge, the very air we breathed saturated in fear, and every footstep felt like the beginning of something worse. When I saw Jax cut through the alley, bloodied but relentless, I knew we couldn't keep this up much longer.

"We've got to find Cairo," I muttered, gritting my teeth. The thought of her being alone out there with the creatures and the grunts both hunting for her made my chest tighten. "Are you good?"

"Radley, I'm fine. Let me go—" Jax started, but I cut him off.

"No, we stay together. She's smarter than this." My tone was more severe than I intended, but they were true. Cairo wasn't a liability. If anything, she was the one who kept us grounded.

But even as I said it, a knot of fear twisted in my stomach. Something was wrong.

Something inside my chest was beating at my ribs, begging me to pay attention.

"Radley!" Mom called from the corner of the street, waving her arms. "We need to clear the square—now!"

The last shadow creature fell with a thud, its dark form dissipating into the night air as the final remnants of its essence vanished. My chest heaved, my body drenched in sweat, but we were finally clearing the streets. The town was slowly, and painfully, finding its balance again.

Jax wiped his bloodied hand on his jeans, panting, his eyes scanning the area. "Where would she go?"

I glanced around, painfully aware of the emptiness in the space beside me. I pushed past a few bodies still moving through the streets, looking for her, calling out her name in desperation. "Cairo?!" The sound of my voice felt wrong in the stillness.

Jax cursed under his breath. "Where the hell did she go?"

"She was right here, Jax," I yelled, pointing toward Cheris's shop as the anxiety built.

I turned on my heel, my mind racing. Where had she gone? My gaze swept over the town square to the darkened streets leading into the heart of Hadeon. She couldn't have gone far, right? I was sure she hadn't just wandered off.

"Let's check Cheris's, then," Jax suggested, his voice low with suspicion. "She was heading that way earlier. Maybe she went in there."

I followed Jax as we rushed down the familiar path to Cheris's tea shop, the adrenaline still coursing through me. The front door was slightly ajar, the bell ringing as we pushed it open.

I called her name, but there was no response.

Jax pushed farther in, scanning the room. "Cheris?"

She appeared from the back of the shop, as calm as ever, a tight smile playing at her lips as though nothing unusual was happening right outside her door.

"Where's Cairo?" I demanded, my voice sharp with frustration.

Cheris's eyes flickered for a moment, a brief glimmer of hesitation before she returned to her usual, composed self. "I don't know," she answered, her tone entirely too controlled. "She hasn't been here."

I stepped closer, a warning in my eyes. "Don't lie to me. She was here. I can smell her on the air, Cheris."

Her face didn't flinch. "I'm afraid I'm not sure where she went. Perhaps she left while you were distracted."

I could hear the faint edge in her voice, a hint of something—something that didn't sit right with me. I scanned the room carefully with my eyes, stopping at the table where a tea cup sat abandoned. A small, delicate thing, with the remnants of tea still inside. And beside it, the white bandages, stained lightly with what I knew had to be Cairo's blood.

My heart dropped. "She was here," I muttered under my breath, my mind racing. I could feel the panic rising in my chest. "What did you do to her?"

Jax stepped forward, his eyes narrowing as he studied the room. "Cheris," he said slowly, his voice cool but laced with an unmistakable threat. "We're not leaving until you tell us what happened."

"I've already told you," she replied evenly, her gaze never leaving mine. "She was here, and then she left. There's nothing else to say."

I didn't believe her. Not for a second.

The muscles in my jaw clenched and I tightened my hand into a fist at my side, but I forced myself to stay calm. "This isn't a fucking game. You don't want to be on the wrong side of this."

Jax moved beside me, adding to the pressure. "You're hiding something. You've always known more than you let on. Now it's time to be honest with us."

She didn't falter, didn't even move. "I've told you all I know. Now, if you don't mind, I have a business to run." Her tone turned polite but firm, a clear dismissal.

I grabbed the edge of the counter, the impulse to lash out clawing at my insides. I took a slow breath, then turned away from her. I didn't have time for this, not now. But I'd be back eventually, and she was going to tell me the truth. I'd make sure of it.

"Where is she?" I growled one last time, but her expression remained as unreadable as ever.

Jax put a hand on my shoulder, pulling me away. He knew I was on the verge of losing my temper. "Let's go. We'll find her."

I wanted to say more, to force her to give me answers, but I knew better. There were bigger problems waiting for us outside.

I took one last look around the room. The smell of Cairo's tea still lingered in the air, a bitter reminder that she'd been here—right here—and now she was gone.

"Radley, you know I can't tell you everything. There are limits to what I can reveal. Just know, things will work out the way they are meant to."

"If a single hair is out of place on her head and I find out you had anything to do with it, I will kill you myself," I promised, my voice low and cold as I turned and walked toward the door. The sudden silence in the shop suffocated me. I could feel Cheris's eyes on my back, the lie she'd told clouding the atmosphere.

Outside, Jax and I both started walking down the street, scanning every corner. We couldn't find her in the square, couldn't find any trace of her anywhere.

My mind raced. What was Cheris hiding? Why wouldn't she tell us what happened? Had something happened to Cairo while I'd been distracted fighting?

We had to find her. And if I had to burn the whole town to the ground to do it, I would.

CHAPTER 44:

CAIRO

The darkness was overwhelming, pressing in on me from all sides. My head felt like it had been split open, the sharp throb at my temples a constant reminder of whatever had knocked me out. I tried to move, but the motion made the dizziness worse, sending a wave of nausea crashing through me. My stomach churned, and I had to take slow, deep breaths to steady myself.

I tried to open my eyes, but the light that pierced the dark seemed too harsh, blinding for a moment. When my vision finally focused, I could see nothing but shadows fluttering just outside the halo of light from the single bulb hanging above me. My heart slammed in my chest. Where was I?

Panic surged through me, and I tensed against the cold metal surface beneath me. I couldn't move. My wrists were bound to the arms of the chair, my ankles tied tightly to the its legs. The ropes were unyielding, cutting into my skin with every small shift. My pulse quickened as I tested the restraints again, but it was useless. Whoever had tied me knew what they were doing.

I pulled harder, gritting my teeth, but the ropes held firm. And then I realized something worse: I couldn't feel the warmth of my magic. The usual hum of power—the familiar connection to the magic flowing through me—was gone. It was like it had been locked away, and the more I strained to reach for it, the further out of my grasp it felt.

It was as though the room itself was closing in all around me, smothering me in the silence. No wind, no sound, just the soft rustle of my own breath. I felt weak. Too weak. It was like something was draining me, slowly sapping whatever strength I had left.

The tea.

My stomach lurched. Of course. The tea Cheris had given me. She'd warned me, but I hadn't listened. She had to have known what it would do.

The way it dulled my senses, numbing my connection to my powers, the same way it silenced everything around me. I had been foolish to trust her.

The old broad actually roofied me? What the fuck is wrong with this town.

But I couldn't think about that now. I needed to focus on getting out of here, on finding a way to escape before whatever was coming found me.

I shifted in the chair again, the rope rubbing my wrists raw at every attempt to loosen them. I couldn't break free, and the longer I sat there, the more the darkness seemed to creep closer. I tried to calm myself, taking deep breaths. My only option was to think.

How had I ended up here? Cheris, the tea, the shadow creatures... then the man. I remembered him watching me from across the street, and I knew it hadn't been a coincidence.

He'd been waiting for me. Waiting for me to be vulnerable.

And of course Anna's platinum-blonde ass was smack dab in the middle of my kidnapping. She always seemed to show up at the worst moments, so why would this be any different?

Then the constable. His face, full of smug certainty as I slipped into unconsciousness. He had been planning this, hadn't he? Had he known I would be drawn to Cheris's shop? He must have. The whole thing had been a trap, a well-set snare designed to catch me.

I closed my eyes, trying to focus through the haze. There had to be a way out. I just needed to find it.

I needed to think. I needed to—

A flare of light cut through the darkness, and my breath caught in my throat. A soft crackling sound, like the flicker of a flame, ignited from the shadows around me. I didn't move, my heartbeat quickening as the dim glow of several candles flared to life in the corners of the room. The light was faint, not nearly enough to banish the darkness entirely, but it was enough to make my senses sharpen. Enough to make me aware that I wasn't alone anymore.

The hairs on the back of my neck prickled, my breath catching in my throat. I could hear footsteps now, soft and measured, approaching from somewhere behind me. I couldn't tell how far away they were, but I could feel the presence, dark and looming.

I forced myself to stay calm despite the fear that clawed at my insides.

The person, whoever they were, was still out of sight. I needed to act quickly, to find a way out before they realized I was awake. But I was still too weak, too dizzy to form a coherent plan. My mind was clouded by the effects of the tea, and the room itself felt like it was swallowing me whole.

I had to try. My magic had to be in there somewhere. I just needed a way to reach it.

Closing my eyes again, I tried to concentrate as I drew in a slow breath. The familiar warmth of my powers—still there, though dulled—tried to respond, but the chains of whatever magic blocked it held firm. The candles wavered, casting eerie shadows across the room, and I pushed harder, trying to break free of the veil that kept me from accessing my magic.

The footsteps grew closer. I could hear the light shuffle of shoes against the floor, and then—there. A voice. Low, soft, almost a whisper, but unmistakable.

"I figured you'd be waking up soon."

The voice was deep, male. Familiar. My pulse skipped.

I forced my head to swivel toward the sound of his voice. The man who had run me and my mother out of Hadeon, the man who'd been willing to sacrifice everything to take my life when I was just a child.

"Why am I here?" My voice was hoarse, cracking slightly, but the words still came out, bitter and defiant.

He chuckled softly. A hollow, mirthless sound.

"You're here because it's time," he said. "Because this is the next step. You and I are connected in ways you don't understand, Cairo. But you will soon enough."

Rage pulsed in the pit of my stomach.

This guy was a fucking sociopath.

With every ounce of strength I could muster, I concentrated again. The power within me stirred, weak at first, but growing stronger with each breath I took. I didn't have much time. If I could just break the bonds, just free my hands enough to—

A flare of light.

The candles around me seemed to pulse brighter, as though responding to my spark of magic I'd managed to muster. I strained harder, pushing, but then everything went black.

The last thing I heard before everything fell into darkness was the constable's cold voice, tinged with a dark satisfaction.

"Everything is in motion, Cairo. And you, my dear, are at the heart of it."

CHAPTER 45:

RADLEY

The night air burned in my lungs as Jax and I sprinted through the streets. Cairo's absence was palpable, like a lead ball in my chest. Every second she was gone felt like an eternity. I couldn't stop picturing her—hurt, scared, alone—and it fueled a rage that boiled just beneath my skin.

"This doesn't make sense," Jax said, his voice tight with frustration. "She wouldn't just disappear."

"She didn't," I barked, barely recognizing my own voice. "The constable has her. He's the only one bold or stupid enough to pull something like this."

We rounded another corner, and that's when I saw him. Trent was leaning against the wall of a shop, scrolling through his phone like nothing in the world mattered. My vision tunneled.

My body moved before I could think.

I grabbed him by the collar, slamming him into the brick wall so hard the air left his lungs with a wheeze. His phone clattered to the ground.

"What the hell, man!" he sputtered, squirming in my grip.

"Where is she?" My voice was ice-cold as I clutched his shirt tighter.

"W-where's who?" he stammered, eyes wide.

"Don't play dumb with me," I growled, shoving him harder against the bricks. "The constable. Where did he take her?"

"I don't-I don't know what you're talking about!"

I jammed my palm against his face, the edge of the wall scraping his cheek as I held him in place. His face contorted in pain, but I didn't care.

"Wrong answer. Try again."

"Radley," Jax said behind me, his voice cautious but firm. "Don't kill him yet. We still need answers."

I ignored him, my focus pinned on Trent's face. "Last chance. Talk."

"I swear, man, I don't know!" His voice cracked, sweat beading on his forehead. "We don't get details like that! The constable keeps his plans to himself!"

I stared at him, my grip tightening, my mind racing. Every instinct screamed to make him suffer for even being connected to this, but he was useless—just another pawn in the constable's game. I let him go, and he crumpled to the ground, gasping for air.

"Get the fuck away from me before I change my mind," I snarled. "And let me make something perfectly clear: if you see Cairo, you better turn around and walk the other way. If you go anywhere near her again, I will rip your limbs from your body and dump the pieces on your mother's doorstep."

Trent scrambled to his feet, nearly tripping over himself as he bolted into the shadows. I turned to Jax, my hands shaking with a fury I had never felt before.

"He doesn't know anything," I gritted out.

"Then we split up," Jax replied without hesitation. "You head back and look through the journals again. If the constable's got her tied to this prophecy crap, there's got to be something we missed. I'll check the town hall. If he's holding her anywhere official, it'll be there."

I nodded. "Call me if you find anything."

"Same to you," Jax said, already turning on his heel and sprinting toward the center of town.

I headed back to my place, adrenaline driving me forward as I tore through the streets.

My father's journals and records had to hold something—a clue, a location, anything. The house was quiet when I burst in, an overwhelming, oppressive silence. I didn't bother turning on the lights as I rushed to the study, ripping through the piles of books and papers we'd barely started to organize. Pages flew to the floor as I searched, my breath coming in ragged gasps.

Then I saw it: a piece of loose-leaf paper, tucked between the pages of an old journal. My heart slammed against my ribs as I read the scribbled handwriting.

"This has got to be it," I whispered to myself desperately. The address was scrawled at the bottom of the note, the ink faded but legible. A single line beneath the address had hope flickering inside me.

"Ritual site of Vaelith."

I grabbed my phone, dialing Jax's number as I raced toward the door. The line rang once, twice, then cut off.

"Damn it!" I cursed, shoving the phone back into my pocket. I didn't have time to waste finding him. Cairo couldn't wait.

I jumped on my motorcycle, the engine roaring to life as I sped toward the address and the note clutched tightly in my hand. I didn't know what else I'd find when I got there, but it didn't matter.

I was going to find her. And I was going to make the constable regret ever laying a fucking hand on my girl.

CHAPTER 46:
CAIRO

My head was pounding, a slow, steady rhythm that made it hard to focus. The room around me was dim, shadows cast by the candles skittering across the basement walls. I couldn't stop the nausea still churning in my stomach, and every breath felt labored, like I was dragging air through mud.

The chair beneath me creaked as I tested the bindings around my wrists again. No give. The rope bit into my skin, twisting my face into a wince as I inadvertently curled my fingers into fists. My magic...I reached for it, desperate for the comforting hum I'd grown used to. Still nothing.

Panic clawed at me, threatening to consume me, but I forced it down. I had to figure out a way out of this.

"I see you're awake again."

The steely voice sliced through the haze cold and sharp. I blinked, lifting my head, and there he was—the constable. He stood a few feet away, hands clasped behind his back, watching me like a predator sizing up its prey.

"Let's see if you can stay that way this time, hmm? You're a hard woman to get alone," he said, his tone almost conversational. "Always surrounded by your little entourage. But I knew this moment would come eventually. It had to."

I glared at him, my voice rasping as I spoke. "What do you want?"

He ignored my question, taking a slow step closer. "I knew the moment I saw your bond to Radley that you would be a problem. And I don't like problems."

I narrowed my eyes, trying to focus through the fog clouding my thoughts. "How did you know about the bond?"

He smiled, a thin, cruel curve of his lips. "I lived next door to you."

The words hit me like a punch to the gut. Next door? My memories of

Hadeon as a child were still fragmented, but I tried to piece them together, searching for some sign of him in the background.

"I saw the whole thing," he continued, his voice dripping with disdain. "From my balcony, I watched as your magic sparked, tying you to that boy. Do you have any idea how rare a bond like that is? How much power it gives you both?"

I didn't answer, my head spinning. He'd known about me all along.

He chuckled darkly, his gaze turning almost nostalgic. "Your mother knew what it meant, of course. She was clever, I'll give her that. The moment she realized I'd seen it, she ran. Packed up and disappeared with you into the night like a thief."

I swallowed hard, my throat dry. "She was protecting me."

"She was delaying the inevitable," he shot back, his voice sharp. "Do you think she didn't know about the prophecy? She was running from that, too. But fate has a way of catching up to people."

"How did you know about the prophecy?" I asked, forcing my voice to stay steady even as my vision blurred.

His smile warped into something more vicious, and he leaned in closer, his face inches from mine. "Because I read it. I found it, just like you did. Though Mr. Cordova's father would disagree with that. A child," he spat, the word dripping with venom, "shouldn't be gifted so much power. So I took it."

I recoiled, his words feeling like a slap across my face. My heart pounded in my chest, the nausea threatening to overwhelm me again.

I couldn't look away from him, his face a mask of cold triumph.

He took it.

"How is that possible?" How can he take power that wasn't given to him by the gods?

He waved his hand in the air dismissively. "We'll get to that part. Right now, I'd like to talk about you. I have a plan for you, girl."

And I had no idea how I was going to stop him. The risk of using my full power without Radley here to anchor me was high. But if I let him win, there was no telling what he would turn this town into.

I couldn't let him run free to save my own life.

He had to be taken down, and every cell in my body knew I was created for that purpose.

"Let's see just how strong that bond is, shall we?"

He raised his hands, and fire erupted beneath my skin.

CHAPTER 47:

RADLEY

The engine roared beneath me as I tore through the winding roads, every twist and turn of the bike feeling like a test of how far I could push myself. The air was sharp and cold against my face, but none of it mattered. My focus was on the bond mark searing into my wrist like a brand, each pulse of pain screaming something is wrong.

I gritted my teeth, clutching the handlebars tighter as my magic flared again, sending bolts of lightning skittering down my arm. It sizzled and roared, zapping my fingers, as if my body was trying to force me to feel her absence.

"Damn it, Cairo," I growled under my breath.

The pain had started as a dull thrum when I'd first realized she was missing. Now it was a full-blown inferno, like the bond itself was on fire. Every nerve ending felt like it was being held to a flame.

The bike skidded slightly as I rounded a sharp curve, and I had to steady myself. My heart was racing, and not just from the speed. I couldn't lose her. Not now.

When I'd first bonded with Cairo, it had been an accident—a kid's reckless desperation to be closer to a friend. I hadn't understood what it meant then. But now, years later, I knew. I felt it in my bones, in my soul. I wasn't just her tether, we were intertwined on a level I don't think I'll ever be able to fully understand.

The mark on my wrist flared again, and I swore loudly, slamming the bike into a higher gear. The closer I got, the worse it burned, like it was trying to guide me toward her. My vision tunneled, a cold sweat covering my body beneath my clothes.

What the fuck was he doing to her? What kind of pain must she be in that I can feel it this far away from her?

I couldn't think about what the constable might have done. I couldn't let myself go there. If I did, I'd lose it.

But the images came anyway. Cairo, tied up, hurt. The constable standing over her with that smug, self-righteous fucking sneer on his face.

Focus.

I forced my mind back to the road, taking deep breaths until my vision evened out. I pleaded with Nytheris to just let me make it to her. My phone buzzed in my pocket, and I almost ignored it, but something told me to check.

With one hand still gripping the handlebars, I yanked it out with the other and glanced at the screen.

Jax.

I cursed and pressed the button to answer, shouting over the wind.

"What?"

"I'm at the town hall," he told me, his voice tight. "Basement's empty. No sign of her. Your mom is here. She keeps saying something about the Veil."

"Then go check it out, but keep looking for her," I barked, the words coming out harsher than I intended.

"You think I'm not?" Jax snapped back. "You're not the only one who gives a damn, Radley."

The bond flared again, cutting through my anger like a knife.

"Fuck, I know," I said, the tremble in my voice softening my tone. "Just—keep me updated."

The call ended, and I shoved the phone back into my pocket. My magic sparked again, the ache in my arm volatile. I couldn't afford to waste time.

Finally, I saw the turnoff ahead for the address I'd found scribbled on that loose piece of paper. My chest burned hotter, the bond pulling me forward with a force I couldn't ignore.

"Hold on, Cairo," I muttered.

I skidded to a stop in front of an abandoned building, the bike's tires kicking up dust. The entire place was dark, rundown and unassuming, like it didn't house the worst kind of danger inside. It looked older than the town, the walls constructed of stone instead of brick, and chunks of the roof were missing.

But I felt her. Somewhere in there, she was waiting for me.

I swung off the bike, my boots hitting the ground with a thud, and strode toward the door. My magic was alive now, crackling around me, pushing at the edges of my control.

If the constable thought he could take her, if he thought he could hurt her— I hoped she would show him exactly what she's capable of.

WHAT LIES BETWEEN US

CHAPTER 48:
CAIRO

The pounding in my head began to subside, replaced by something else—something deep and steady, like the thrum of an unseen current. I kept my breathing slow, steady, though every instinct screamed at me to panic. My fingers flexed against the rope digging into my skin, and as I closed my eyes for a moment, I felt it. A faint hum, like a thread stretching out just within my reach. My magic was returning.

I opened my eyes, forcing my gaze back to the constable. He stood a few feet away, arms crossed, watching me like I was some puzzle he'd finally solved.

The burning feeling receded, whatever magic he had used to cause me pain finally seeping back into his hands as he spoke.

"Did you ever wonder," he began, his voice deceptively calm, "why there were two prophecies?"

I blinked, trying to keep him talking while I focused on the threads of magic flickering back to life inside me. "I don't know what you're talking about."

He snickered darkly, shaking his head. "Don't play dumb, Cairo. You're smarter than that. The prophecy about you—the one your mother knew about—was only half the story.

There's another. One the rest of the town doesn't even know exists."

I kept my expression neutral, though my heart was pounding. "Why would I believe you?"

"You don't have to," he answered, his tone turning sharp. "But you'll want to. You see, the first prophecy was written by the Nytheris. It foretold someone like you. A savior, they'd call you, though I find that a bit dramatic. The second prophecy, though...that one was mine to fulfill."

"Yours?" I scoffed, trying to buy myself time as the hum of my magic grew louder, more insistent. Slowly, carefully, I began to work the threads of my power into the bindings around my wrists.

"You see, Vaelith and Nytheris, neither of them trusted the other to play fair," he continued, his voice almost mocking, "so they each wrote their own prophecy. The second prophecy was precaution. A failsafe, if you will. And guess what? I made sure I'd be the one to claim it."

I gritted my teeth, pulling at the threads of magic, weaving them into the rope. "You made a bargain."

He smiled, cold and calculating. "A very advantageous one. As it turns out, Vaelith wasn't picky about who fulfilled the role, so long as someone did. And why shouldn't it be me? Power like that shouldn't belong to a child."

I froze for a moment, my mind racing. "You bargained for the prophecy?"

He leaned closer, his voice dropping. "I did. And all I had to do to claim it was ensure the first prophecy didn't come to pass. Simple, really."

"You were going to kill me," I said, my voice shaking despite my efforts to keep it steady.

"I still am," he replied matter-of-factly. "Kill you, here, on sacred grounds, and the power is mine. But now, I realize I've underestimated you. You're not the only one tied to this. That bond of yours complicates things."

My stomach twisted. "Radley."

He smirked, catching the panic in my voice. "If I can't kill you to stop it, I'll just have to kill you both."

"No!" The word tore from my throat, and I yanked at the bindings, magic surging through me in a desperate attempt to break free. The rope resisted, but I could feel it weakening, fibers straining as I poured everything I had into unraveling it.

He stepped back, watching me with an almost amused look on his face. "You're worried about him," he said. "Good. It'll make what comes next even more satisfying."

I glared at him, my breath ragged as I worked faster, my magic burning brighter with every passing second.

"You're a coward," I spat. "You couldn't stomach the thought of someone else having more power than you, so you stole it. And now you're afraid of me."

His expression darkened, and for the first time, I saw a flash of some-thing—doubt, maybe?

"Afraid of you?" he repeated, his tone icy. "You think I don't know what you are? Who you are?"

I froze, my magic faltering for a split second. "What are you talking about?"

He took a step closer, his eyes boring into mine. "Your mother kept secrets, Cairo. She was good at that. But she couldn't hide everything."

"What secrets?" I demanded, though my voice was barely above a whisper.

He crouched down so we were eye level, his next words like a punch to the gut. He clicked his tongue at me, forcing his face into a mask of sympathy. "I'm your father."

The world seemed to tilt, the air sucked from the room. My hands went still, the magic working to unravel the ropes faltering as his words sank in.

"You're lying," I whispered.

His smirk returned, though there was something bitter in it. "Believe what you want. But she ran from me because she knew the truth. She knew I wouldn't let her keep you hidden forever."

"No." My voice came out stronger this time. "She ran because you're a monster."

His laugh was sharp and humorless. "Maybe. But that doesn't change the fact that you're mine. She knew that, and if she had any sense at all, she would have known you would never get away from me. Not forever."

Something inside me snapped. The shock, the fear, the confusion—all of it melted away, replaced by a blinding, burning rage. My magic surged, stronger than before, and with one final push, the ropes around my wrists fell away.

The constable's eyes widened in surprise, but I was already moving, the chair screeching against the floor as I stood. My legs were shaky, my vision swimming, but I didn't care.

"You want my life? Fucking fight me for it," I said, my voice low and steady.

For the first time, I saw something in his eyes that looked like fear. But he quickly masked it, stepping back as if to put distance between us.

"You don't have the strength," he retorted, though his voice lacked the confidence it had before.

I didn't answer. I didn't need to. My magic pulsed around me, a wild, untamed force that I couldn't fully control but refused to suppress any longer.

"Come see how strong I am for yourself."

I didn't know how this would end, but I knew one thing for sure.

He was wrong.

I had the strength.

CHAPTER 49:
CAIRO

The constable paced slowly in front of me, his boots scuffing against the cold stone floor as he watched me with beady eyes. My muscles screamed from the strain of pulling at my binds earlier, but I refused to show any weakness. My magic simmered beneath my skin, a low hum of returning power, but I only had one chance at surprising him. He was bigger than me, and between the two of us I had no idea who was more powerful.

He smirked, his expression maddeningly calm, as if we weren't circling each other like predators ready to strike.

"You must know, Cairo, this isn't personal," he said, his tone deceptively nonchalant. "It's just…you're in my way."

"Right. Kidnapping and attempted murder? Nothing personal at all." My voice dripped with sarcasm, but I kept my stance fixed, my hands clenched at my sides. The room still felt too small, the air too thick, my head still throbbing from whatever Cheris had put in that tea.

He chuckled, an infuriating sound that made my fingers twitch with the urge to lash out.

"Don't misunderstand me. I respect what you've done—surviving this long, coming back here, stirring things up. But you were never meant to win this."

The air around us shifted, shadows sliding along the wall behind him making him appear larger. I saw the flicker of magic in his hands a second before he moved, and I barely had time to throw my hands up before the first blast hit.

The impact sent me stumbling back, but I dug my heels in, forcing my magic to rise to the surface. Darkness swarmed at the edge of my vision, curling around me like a living thing.

"Still think you can win this?" the constable taunted, sending another wave of energy my way.

I dodged, the blast grazing my shoulder, and countered with a surge of shadows that lashed out toward him. He deflected them easily, batting them away like gnats as his smirk grew.

"You're strong, I'll give you that," he said, circling me again. "But strength isn't enough."

"I guess we'll find out," I shot back, forcing another wave of magic his way. My arms shook from the effort it took to release the power I'd worked so hard to control. I noticed the rope burns circling both of my wrists as I held my hands out, thin ribbons of blood dripping slowly onto the floor at my feet.

That's a tomorrow problem, Cairo. Focus.

We clashed again and again, the room trembling with the force of our attacks. My head was still spinning, but my magic was stronger now, the shadows swirling around me like armor. I forced air into my lungs, breathing deeply and planting my feet firmly on the concrete floor. How long would that tea last?

Note to self: beat Cheris's ass after this.

There was only one way to get the upper hand. If I needed Radley, then there was no way he was using the full extent of his power, not without an anchor. He was too self-absorbed to ever risk his life, even if it meant taking mine. The arrogance oozing out of him told me everything I needed to know.

He thought I was weak enough that he could take me out, and only expend a portion of his power to do it.

I exhaled sharply, stealing a precious moment to close my eyes and dive toward the source of my power. That burning fire in the depths of my chest that called to me and terrified me in equal measure. I would not let this man walk out of here. I couldn't.

The idea of him returning to town, his power far outweighing anyone else's, I couldn't bear it. He would go after Radley and Jax, and who knows who else.

He wasn't just a danger to me, he was a danger to anyone that crossed his path.

This was my purpose. This is why Nytheris chose me.

Finding the thick stream of magic coiled inside me, I yanked at it with all of my strength, dragging it to the surface as my eyes shot open.

My skin flared, golden light pulsing beneath my flesh as the magic took over.

"The difference between you and me is that I am willing to die as long as I take you with me."

I pushed the power out of me, a wave of bright light erupting from my body and slamming the constable against the stone walls. His eyes widened in panic, his mouth sputtering to form words.

With each second I could feel the power tearing at the muscle and sinew inside me, ripping tendons from bone and searing my flesh.

It's worth it. They'll be safe.

I bit back a scream as I encouraged the power to grow, splitting it into a steady stream of fire that raced up his legs and a beam of golden light that pierced into his body just above his stomach.

I willed it to go deeper, to sink into him and find the rot and decay and stolen magic and rip it out by the root.

His screams were drowned out by my own.

I can't do this much longer…

The searing pain was easing into a prickling numbness, though sweat ran in rivers down my spine and my arms were shaking uncontrollably.

The constable raised a shaking hand, his arm vibrating with the effort of delivering another strike, but before he could release it, the door burst open, slamming against the wall with a deafening crash.

"Cairo!" Radley's voice roared through the chaos, and my heart leaped at the sound.

The relief was short lived as he called my name again, but he was standing right in front of me.

Why does he sound like he's underwater? That can't be a good sign.

The constable turned his head, his face contorting with rage, but I didn't give him a chance to react. With a surge of desperation, I let the shadows consume me, letting them explode outward in a wave of darkness that engulfed the entire room.

The constable's shout was drowned out by the roar of my magic, the light and fire flooding back into me in a painful current that knocked me

off my feet.
And then, there was nothing but darkness.

WHAT LIES BETWEEN US

CHAPTER 50:
RADLEY

I hit my knees, catching Cairo as her body crumpled to the floor. Reaching through the swirling darkness, my fingers found her hip and pulled her firmly to me. The moment I made contact, the suffocating shadows she'd unleashed became something I could see through, clear as day. Her face was tight with concentration, her chest heaving from exertion. I pushed the damp hair back from her face, noting the swelling around her left eye where someone had landed a blow.

"Cairo? Baby open your eyes, look at me," I begged, leaning in, my voice low.

She groaned in my arms, her lips pressed together tightly, but her eyes flew open. The vulnerability in her gaze gutted me.

"I'm okay," she whispered, her voice shaky and raw.

My eyes shifted to the constable, who was staggering in the black haze, disoriented and gasping. My blood boiled at the sight of him. His audacity, his cruelty, his smugness that had burned in my mind since the first day he looked at her. I kissed the top of Cairo's head, carefully lowering her to the floor. "I'll be right back, sweetheart." I stood and stalked toward him, the fury in my veins igniting my magic.

I didn't hesitate. My fist connected with his jaw, sending him reeling into the stone wall behind him. Before he could recover, I hit him again, pouring my power into every strike. The shadows vibrated with energy around us, amplifying every blow.

It wasn't enough. He deserved worse. He deserved everything I could fucking give him for what he did to her. The purple bruising around her eye was seared into my mind, my jaw locked tight as I swung again and again, feeling bones crack against my knuckles.

I shoved his hands away as he reached for me, hurling him against the wall with a pulse of magic. Blood streaked his mouth, and his grunts of pain only fueled my rage.

I wrapped my hand around his throat and held him against the wall, ramming my knee into his stomach before leaning in close.

"What kind of pathetic little bitch puts his hands on a woman?" I whispered in his ear, my voice tight with anger. "And how fucking stupid do you have to be to touch *that one*?" I dug my nails into the flesh around his eye, the same side he had bruised on Cairo, and twisted my fingers, pushing deeper until I felt bone and then yanking my hand free.

He fell to the ground, a scream clawing its way out of his throat as he clutched at his face.

"Get the fuck up." I landed a solid kick to his exposed ribs, reveling in the way he curled into a ball at my feet.

"Radley." Cairo's voice broke through the haze of anger, a steadying force even now. I paused, my chest heaving as I turned to her. She had managed to get to her feet and was walking over to me with a painful-looking limp.

"Do you want me to finish it?" I asked, stepping back and letting the constable slump to the ground.

She shook her head, her expression cold and unflinching as she approached. Her hands were raised, power radiating from her in waves, the darkness swirling tighter around us.

"I need answers from him first."

The constable laughed—a horrible, wet sound through the blood pouring from his mouth. His one good eye flicked to Cairo, his lips curling into a mocking grin as a river of blood oozed from his eye socket.

"You think it ends here?" he rasped, his voice dripping with defiance. "The prophecy will just move to the one it was originally intended for."

Cairo froze, her shadows twitching in the air around her before evaporating altogether. She whipped her head toward me, her eyes wide with alarm.

"Say hello to your brother for me." He smiled, bloodied teeth on full display.

"What does that mean?" I demanded, stepping closer, my fists clenched.

The constable's laugh turned into a hacking cough, but he managed to choke out the words. He gestured weakly toward me, his bloody grin growing. "Oh, that's good. You really have no idea who the other chosen one is, do you?"

"Who?" Cairo demanded, her voice sharp and unyielding.

He didn't answer, his body shuddering as the life began to leave him.

"Tell us!" I shouted, slamming my foot against the ground near his head, but the constable only sneered.

"You'll find out soon enough," he wheezed. "Better catch him quick, though. That rush of power is strong enough to snuff out any light he has in him."

His head lolled to the side, his body shuddering and then going limp as the last wheezing breath left him.

The room fell silent, save for the crackling of residual magic and our own ragged breathing. Cairo stood frozen, her shadows coiling and uncoiling around her palms in the dim light. I stepped forward, wiping the blood from my hands on my jeans before gently tucking her against me.

"He was fucking with us, Cai," I said, though the unease in my chest told me he wasn't. Cairo didn't answer, her gaze fixed on the constable's lifeless body. The implication of his words was stifling. We didn't know who the other chosen one was—but we were running out of time to figure it out.

CHAPTER 51:

JAX

I grabbed my keys from the counter, my mind already racing toward Radley and Cairo. I had to get to them. Something wasn't right, and it gnawed at me like a dull ache in my chest. There were grunts all over town, and I could feel the pull of the constable's twisted influence closing in on us. I made a quick stop at my house to grab a power bank, plugging it into my phone while hoping and praying Radley had found her and left a message before my phone died on me.

I'd spent the last twenty minutes at the town border with Vesper and a group of elders. The Veil was waning. Ripples ran across its surface, something I had never seen before, and apparently no one else had either. Panic erupted within the crowd that had gathered at the edge of town, no one understanding what was happening or what it meant.

It wasn't a great sign.

The Veil was the only thing keeping our little town a secret. If it fell, I had no idea what would happen here.

I swung my keys around by the ring, the cool metal sliding smoothly along my finger, I made it three steps toward the driveway before I felt it—a pressure building behind my eyes. A strange dizziness that made the world tilt and spin.

I blinked, trying to clear the haze from my vision. Spots danced in my line of sight, like a thousand little stars crashing into the edges of my periphery. My pulse quickened, hammering in my ears as my hands began to tremble. I couldn't focus.

What the fuck is this?

I swayed, my knees threatening to buckle beneath me, but I caught myself against the wall, pressing my palms to the cool surface. It helped for a moment, before my heart picked up speed, thudding in my chest like a war drum. I stumbled back into the house and toward the bathroom, the hallway shifting in and out of focus as my breaths grew shallow.

Splashing cold water on my face was supposed to help. That's what I always did when things got bad—when my head felt like it was going to explode, when the world seemed to fall apart around me.

I cupped my hands and tossed frigid water on my face, over and over again.

But this time, the water did nothing. The dizziness only grew worse, and the tremors in my hands became more violent.

Fuck. Fuck. Fuck.

I fumbled for my phone on the edge of the sink, my fingers slick and shaky as I tried to dial Radley's number. Nothing. The screen blurred and shifted in my hands, and the harder I tried to focus, the more everything seemed to slip away from me.

My hands were burning.

I opened my palms in front of me, the heat crawling up my arms and spreading through my body. The pain was sharp, like something searing me from the inside out. My veins felt like they were full of gasoline. I gritted my teeth, trying to breathe through it, but it was useless. I couldn't escape the flames that seemed to curl and twist under my skin.

My vision faltered.

One second, the bathroom was clear, and the next, everything was shrouded in darkness. I stumbled forward, smacking my palm against the wall to steady myself. My breath came in ragged gasps, desperate and panicked as the world spun faster than I could follow. I could hear the wet wheezes coming from my mouth, the sound heightening the already growing panic inside me.

Beneath my palms, I could feel something writhing, moving under my flesh and coiling along every inch of exposed skin on my body. I pried my eyes open, my mouth falling slack as I examined the thick black cords that squirmed under my skin.

Thick, dark tendrils of ink sprouted from somewhere deep inside me, surfacing where my veins should be and traveling up my body, curving around my shoulders and resting around my neck like tattoos.

Then, just as quickly as it had started, it stopped.

Everything snapped back into focus. My vision cleared, and the world was back, the room sharp and distinct. But something was wrong. Something fundamental to who I am shifted inside of me. Pieces broke off, something new molding itself to the chipped places and cementing itself there.

I lifted my head, my chest heaving with the effort to draw a steady breath, and looked into the mirror.

The reflection staring back at me wasn't mine—not entirely.

My eyes were solid black.

A deep, inky void where my irises should've been, empty and endless. The blackness seemed to swirl, like something alive, pulsing and growing as I stared into the mirror. My heart skipped a beat, a cold shiver running down my spine.

What the hell is happening to me?

I swallowed hard, my mouth dry. I reached up, touching my face, my trembling fingers brushing against my skin like it wasn't even my own. The burning in my hands was still there, but now it felt different—stronger.

I felt the pull of something else inside of me, something dark and powerful, and it terrified me.

But somewhere, somewhere deep, beneath the fear, there was a hunger.

And power like I had never known.

To be continued...

www.ingramcontent.com/pod-product-compliance
Lightning Source LLC
Chambersburg PA
CBHW050317110726
47899CB00007B/2272